A Dragon's Guide to Making your Human Smarter

Also by Laurence Yep and Joanne Ryder

A Dragon's Guide to the Care and Feeding of Humans

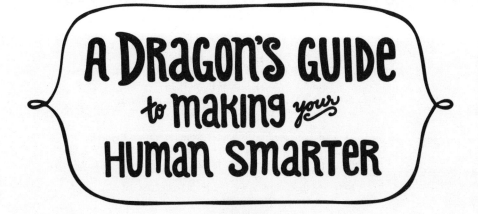

A Dragon's Guide to Making your Human Smarter

Book 2

Laurence Yep & Joanne Ryder

Illustrations by Mary GrandPré

CROWN BOOKS
FOR YOUNG READERS
NEW YORK

Text copyright © 2016 by Laurence Yep and Joanne Ryder
Jacket art and interior illustrations copyright © 2016 by Mary GrandPré

The following poems appear in this book:
James Russell Lowell, "The Falcon," originally published as "The Falconer"
in *The Liberty Bell,* December 1845.
Gerard Manley Hopkins, "The Windhover," *Poems of Gerard Manley Hopkins*
(London: Humphrey Milford, 1918).
John Gillespie Magee, Jr., "High Flight," first published
in the Pittsburgh *Post-Gazette,* November 12, 1941.

Visit us on the Web! randomhousekids.com

Educators and librarians, for a variety of teaching tools, visit us at
RHTeachersLibrarians.com

Library of Congress Cataloging-in-Publication Data
Yep, Laurence.
A dragon's guide to making your human smarter / Laurence Yep & Joanne Ryder ;
illustrations by Mary GrandPré. — First edition.
pages cm. — (A dragon's guide ; 2)
Summary: Winnie is challenged to adapt to a new school for girls where teaching
is anything but ordinary and where the eclectic student body includes magicals
as well as humans, and while Winnie uses her wits to find her own way,
crusty dragon Miss Drake is secretly trying to discover and foil a new plot
by Winnie's grandfather to gain custody of her.
ISBN 978-0-385-39232-7 (trade) — ISBN 978-0-385-39233-4 (lib. bdg.) —
ISBN 978-0-385-39235-8 (pbk.) — ISBN 978-0-385-39234-1 (ebook)
[1. Schools—Fiction. 2. Dragons—Fiction. 3. Magic—Fiction.] I. Ryder, Joanne,
author. II. GrandPré, Mary, illustrator. III. Title.
PZ7.Y44Dqrk 2016 [Fic]—dc23 2015010892

Printed in the United States of America
10 9 8 7 6 5 4 3 2 1
First Edition

To Zander Salinas,
wishing you wonderful adventures and journeys,

and in memory of Darlene Abdale,
remarkable teacher and beloved friend

CHAPTER ONE

Unless you are willing to keep your pet safe and make your pet smarter, collect stamps instead.

MISS DRAKE

I thought Winnie looked quite fetching in her new uniform and said so.

She drew her eyebrows together in puzzlement. "Fetching?"

"Pretty, winsome—like your name," I explained.

She plucked at the hem of her blue-and-black plaid skirt. "You don't think the uniforms are sort of old-fashioned?"

"It speeds up socialization when you can skip criticizing one another's clothes and can go directly to criticizing one another's characters," I said. "Just be grateful you're not wearing bloomers."

The wrinkled forehead again. "Bloomers?"

"They were pants girls used to wear in physical education. They made you look like you were wearing a deflated balloon," I said.

She sighed. "Sometimes I need subtitles when you talk."

"Don't be silly," I said. "The whole point of going to school is to learn enough so you can understand me."

"I still say subtitles would be easier," she said, and pointed at the tablet in my hand. "After school, when I come back, I'll find a translation app for you."

I raised my tablet out of her reach. "The last time I let you touch my tablet, I got it back full of games."

Winnie was an impudent little thing. "You need to have more fun. You don't smile enough. You look beautiful when you smile."

"A dragon is beautiful simply by being a dragon," I sniffed. "It should be obvious."

The corner of Winnie's mouth crooked up skeptically. "Of course."

Though it may be unusual for a dragon to have a pet human, I enjoy doing so. I pride myself on training them well.

Sarcasm does not become a pet and I would normally

have corrected her attitude, but it was just before her first day at the Spriggs Academy. "Now run along. You don't want to be late."

Still she lingered. "I'll be home before you know it."

"I'll count the minutes," I said drily.

Winnie took me literally, though. "I'll miss you too." And she wrapped her arms around as much of me as she could. "This has been the best summer ever."

I patted her carefully on the back, because naturals are such fragile little things. "It's been the best summer for me too."

When she stepped away, I saw that she had hugged me so tightly that my scales had left faint impressions on her cheek. "I put those other games on your tablet so you could play them while I'm gone. I know you've been doing them, because I check your scores when you aren't looking." She added, "You're getting better, but you're not up to my level yet."

"You've got some nerve." We could definitely use some time apart.

She started to open the door but then turned around. "Will I really be okay at Spriggs?"

It was my turn to misunderstand. Her grandfather Jarvis had been trying to take Winnie away from her mother, Liza. Winnie's schooling had been haphazard as a result.

"You're smart," I assured her. "You'll fill any gaps in your education in no time, and if you're having problems, tell me and we'll hire the best tutors."

She frowned. "No, I mean I'm a human, but a lot of kids there will be magicals."

I raised a claw, and to her credit, Winnie didn't even flinch. Gently, I rubbed out the lines my scales had left on her face. "Spriggs is for both naturals and magicals." The naturals were usually the children of families who did business with the magicals, and for the last five generations, Spriggs had been preparing both for an often unkind world. "And you come from a family famous among magicals."

She wrinkled her forehead a third time. "What's my family famous for?"

"Being friends with me, of course," I said.

She rolled her eyes—at least that was more like her usual self. "Why don't I just make a sign and wear it?" Her fingers traced the invisible words. *"I know Miss Drake."*

"A sensible suggestion," I said, opening the door with one paw and shoving her outside with the other. "But it's not in the dress code."

My apartment is hidden in the mansion's basement, where my front door opens on what looks like an old, unused storage room.

I listened to Winnie's steps fade, slow and reluctant at first but then quicker—as if she had finally worked up the courage to face the day.

As I said, I was looking forward to having time alone, but I had much to do before she left our house. I glanced again at the warning that my lawyer and friend, Dylis, had emailed me yesterday.

> Now that Winnie's grandfather Jarvis can't seek custody of her because her mother is no longer poor, I've heard rumors that he's either hired someone to grab his granddaughter or uncovered something else he can use to get her instead. Stick close to her until I can find out more.

Dylis had moles everywhere, and she claimed that, as a dwarf, she knew good dirt from bad. So I took all her warnings seriously.

I forwarded the email to my foxy friend and computer geek, Reynard, and added the question:

> Can you help?

Reynard was at his computer as usual. Naturally.

Do it. Find out who and what I'm up against.

After enlisting one of the cleverest beings I knew, it was time to take the next step.

Jarvis thought he could still pick on Winnie and her mother. He didn't realize that they had a dragon on their side.

....

∽ Winnie ∽

Dragons are the most fun you'll ever have, and dragons are the most trouble too, especially one as grumpy as Miss Drake. My family has owned her for five generations now, and so far we'd kept her from biting anyone's head off—at least that we knew about.

I always thought that Great-Aunt Amelia had been making up stories in her letters about Miss Drake, so I didn't know what to believe when I got her last one. Not only was the dragon real, but my aunt wanted me to take care of her precious pet!

Great-Aunt Amelia was so old that at first I thought she had begun to think her imaginary adventures had actually happened. But when I went to the hidden apartment in the basement, there was Miss Drake—scales, bad temper, and all.

Still, no matter how mean Miss Drake talked, I could always get her to show her marshmallow side. She took me flying, and we'd had all sorts of super adventures together. Though I'd only met her a month ago, I felt like we'd been together all my life—maybe because of all the stories Great-Aunt Amelia had written to me.

School's starting, and I felt really, really bad about leaving Miss Drake all alone in that big old house. What was she going to do without me cheering her up all day?

So make it up to her after school, I told myself. I'd play checkers with her, and I'd even let her win a game for a change.

I climbed the steps from the basement and smelled the wonderful aromas coming from the kitchen.

When I entered, I saw Vasilisa taking a tray from the stove. "Good morning, Little Madame."

Vasilisa was both our cook and our housekeeper. She was about thirty. Her blond hair was in a tight bun at the back of her head, and under her apron she wore a lavender dress with large embroidered red roses along the hem. Miss Drake knew all about her. She said that Vasilisa's family had worked here for generations.

"Morning," I said, "and I wish you'd call me Winnie."

A title didn't feel right for someone who had been living in a trailer two months ago.

Vasilisa didn't refuse outright. She just smiled patiently. In her own way, she could be almost as stubborn as Miss Drake.

"You are just in time," Vasilisa said, setting the tray on the kitchen table. "I have just made fresh croissants with Black Forest ham and Gruyère cheese inside."

On the windowsill was Vasilisa's doll, half-turned so she could look at the kitchen and the backyard at the same time. When she wasn't there, she was usually inside a pocket on Vasilisa's apron.

Taking off her oven mitts, Vasilisa carefully cut off a bit of a croissant. Cheese bubbled and oozed out, and Vasilisa eased a spatula under the piece and slid it onto a small plate. Putting the dish on the windowsill in front of her doll, she said, "Small Doll, Small Doll, you must be hungry."

Then she took a thimble-size porcelain cup and very carefully poured a couple drops of coffee into it from the pot. Placing the cup by the dish, Vasilisa murmured, "Small Doll, Small Doll, you must be thirsty."

The doll's painted eyes suddenly gleamed like diamonds, and the next moment, the piece of croissant and the coffee had disappeared.

"I never get tired of watching her do that," I said.

"And she never gets tired of watching you—especially since you give her you-know-what." Vasilisa used the spatula to put another croissant on a dish and held it out to me.

"Thanks." It was delicious, like all of Vasilisa's baking and cooking.

It was Vasilisa's doll that did all the cleaning, dusting, and laundry at night while Vasilisa slept in her room here. A couple of times I tried to stay up long enough to catch the doll at it, but somehow I always fell asleep before that happened.

The doll, though, must have said something to Vasilisa, because one day, she explained, "Little Madame, it is no good peeking. She will never let you see her at work, only when she is at rest and ready for company. There is a time and place for everything, you know?"

I knew by then that the doll ate stuff, so I asked, "Is there anything she especially likes?"

Vasilisa glanced down at her pocket, and then leaned in close to whisper in my ear. "She loves c-h-o-c-o-l-a-t-e."

"Choco—?" I began, when Vasilisa clapped a hand over my mouth. Her fingers smelled a little like flour.

"Shh, never say that word," Vasilisa warned me. "It

won't last here, because she eats it all. She loves it as much as she loves me and this house."

I glanced down and thought I saw the doll's round wooden head poking out of the pocket, painted eyes turned up toward me.

So the next day, I'd gotten a chocolate bar and gone into the kitchen, where Vasilisa was stirring something in a big pot. "Vasilisa, I'll leave a little gift on the table for her."

But when I put my hand in my coat pocket, it was empty. "It's gone."

Vasilisa added a pinch of pepper to the pot. "No you-know-what lasts long in this house when she smells it, but it is a good thing you offered it to her. Now she will make your life as sweet as the candy bar you bought her. And if you ever need her wisdom or help, she will give it as freely as the treat you gave her."

As of this morning, though, I hadn't needed anything from Small Doll that she wasn't already doing for me.

Vasilisa handed me a cloth napkin. Embroidered in one corner were three dragons like the weather vane on top of our house. "And now you have both eaten, she will go with you, Little Madame."

I wiped my mouth and hands. "Why would she want to go to school?" I wasn't sure what the other kids would say if they saw me with a doll.

Vasilisa shrugged. "Perhaps she is curious." She raised an eyebrow. "But she is very definite about going. You will do her this kindness, please?"

I thought of all that Vasilisa's doll did for us. "Sure," I said.

Vasilisa looked a little nervous as I went to the windowsill. When was the last time she and her doll had been apart?

"I'll take good care of her," I promised. I picked up the doll respectfully and put her in my pocket.

Vasilisa put another croissant into a ziplock bag, which she slipped into a nylon bag. It was green with horseshoes on it. "Tell Madame that her lunch is in this bag along with her breakfast." There was also a red one with stars. "I made your lunch too. Last night I asked Madame what drinks I should pack for you and her, and she said she would tell me, but then she never did. So I put in juice cartons for you both."

I picked up the lunches. "Sorry. Mom's got a lot on her mind."

"And so do you, Little Madame." Vasilisa dipped her head. "But do not worry. Small Doll will be with you."

I'd just stepped back into the hallway, when I heard Mom calling from the second floor, "Winnie? Winnie? Where are you?"

"Down here, Mom," I said.

Mom limped down the steps. "I don't want either of us to be late today."

She was wearing riding boots, jeans, and Dad's old sweater. It was a couple of sizes too big for her, and she had to roll up the sleeves. No matter how many times we had washed it, it still had a big blue splotch. When I was small, I used to keep my eyes on it as he walked through the fields looking for a spot that would inspire him to paint.

She stopped three steps above me, one hand holding up the camera she had bought yesterday. "Say 'cheese.'"

"Cheese." I stretched up the corners of my mouth as much as I could.

She snapped a picture. "Okay, now that you got that out of your system, how about a real smile?"

"Only if I get one of you," I said, putting down the lunch bags.

When she took the second picture, she handed me the camera, and I took one of her still on the staircase. "We'll call this *The Lady of the Manor*."

"I don't feel like one." Mom limped down the steps, looking around the long hallway with the fancy molding and pictures on the wall. "It still all seems like a dream. Thank you, Aunt Amelia."

"I wish I'd gotten to meet her," I said.

Mom pocketed the camera. "I only met her when I was small, so all I remember is that she was a lot of fun. It drove my dad crazy."

I handed the green bag to Mom. "Here's your lunch. And for breakfast, there's a yummy croissant with ham and cheese."

As Mom took her lunch, she shook her head. "Vasilisa's a real marvel, isn't she? She not only cooks but also keeps this big place spotless. It's almost like magic."

It is magic, Mom, I thought. It was killing me not to tell Mom about Miss Drake or the oodles of magic around us. But I had promised Miss Drake not to until she decided it was safe to let Mom in on the whole truth.

"Yeah, amazing," I said as Mom pecked my cheek and then gave me a quick hug.

"Sure you don't want me to give you a lift to school?" she asked.

"Mom, it's only eight blocks away," I protested, and adjusted the folds of her sleeves. "Anyway, I wish you wouldn't rush back to work. It's not like we need the money."

"I'd go stir-crazy, Win," Mom assured me. "The job's only part-time, and even then my duties are going to be light. I'll stay in the office. I won't be teaching now.

Rhiannon's been really sweet." Rhiannon was the owner of the stables by Half Moon Bay where Mom worked.

"The doctor said only short rides, remember." When Mom was healthy, she would've spent most of her time in the saddle if she could. "I won't be there to keep an eye on you. So promise me you won't overdo it."

After Dad had died, it had just been the two of us. I had watched over Mom, and she had watched over me. When she could, Mom had worked as a practice rider or took whatever jobs she could get at stables, but sometimes she had waitressed or bagged groceries so she could feed us.

When she had hurt her leg and couldn't work anymore, we hadn't known how we were going to pay our bills. Then a miracle had happened, and Great-Aunt Amelia left us her house and all her stuff as well as Dylis, a first-class lawyer. Our legal problems went poof, and I got a dragon of my very own.

"Please swear you'll take care of yourself," I begged. "I'll be too busy worrying about you to keep my mind on my classes."

"I won't overdo it if you swear you'll let me know me if anyone tries to bully you." Mom wagged a finger in front of my nose. "No more settling things on your own."

Because we'd been on the run from my grandfather,

I'd switched schools a lot, and sometimes I met jerks who thought they'd try to pick on me. At one place, a kid had pushed me too far.

"It was only a black eye," I said.

"But if your granddad hears about a fight, he might use it as proof that I'm a bad parent," Mom said.

The thought of Granddad trying to get me again was scary enough, but I'd lose Miss Drake too. I couldn't let that happen. I mean, what would she do without me? "Sure, I'll behave."

"And when in doubt, ask yourself what I would do."

"Okay, you got a deal, Mom," I said.

I'd left my backpack by the front door. I put my lunch inside it, then shrugged my arms through its straps. My textbooks were a heavy load. I had to lean forward slightly to balance myself.

The funny thing was that as I soon as I stepped outside, I had this feeling someone was looking at me. I turned to see if it was Mom with one last warning, but the door was shut. And now I sensed the watcher was in front of me. I tried to whirl around to catch whoever it was, but I hadn't allowed for the load on my back. I started to fall like a cut tree.

I waved my arms frantically, but I knew I was going to land hard.

Suddenly I stopped.

"Got you, Miss Winnie." A strong reddish-brown hand grabbed my arm and held me steady until I could stand on my own.

"Thanks, Paradise," I said. She was the gardener who took care of everything outside the house. It was strange to have one when we'd never had any yard before.

Dylis had given Vasilisa and Paradise some time off after my great-aunt's funeral. So we didn't meet them until their return. When Miss Drake introduced us, she told me that Paradise was a dryad from a redwood tree up north but she now lived here in a transplanted sapling from her original tree. You couldn't tell from the way she dressed in regular brown overalls and big, clunky rubber boots. The only real hint was the faint green color at the roots of her black hair.

"Straighten up, miss, or you'll grow at a twisty angle," she advised me.

"Can't help it. The load makes me tilt," I said as I started down our driveway.

When I got to the gate at the end, I paused.

Okay, Winnie, it's jump time, I told myself.

After Dad had died, Mom had been the only thing I could count on. Everything kept changing all the time. New towns. New schools. Always having to start over again. I finally quit trying to make friends.

16

Whenever we moved, Mom called it jumping out of a plane and hitting the ground running. We'd gotten good at it.

So I took a breath and jumped for the very last time. When I felt my shoes land on the pavement, I let out a big laugh. The Spriggs Academy, here I come!

All I had to do was head two blocks south across the hilltop and then turn east and walk six blocks. Along my way, I saw other girls in uniforms like mine.

I glanced at them, trying to figure out who were humans and who were magicals. I guessed the girl wearing the big wide-brimmed hat and heavy-duty sunscreen might be a vampire—but she could also have been a human who sunburned easily.

I wondered how the magical kids would treat me. For that matter, what would the human kids think of me?

The Spriggs Academy took up two city blocks in one of the fanciest neighborhoods in the city. Miss Drake told me that one of the early gold rush millionaires had built it as a home. When he went bust in 1860, the Academy had taken it over and added to it through the years.

An iron fence surrounded the school. Decorating the center of each post was a small gargoyle. It was strange: their eyes seemed to follow me as I passed them. Beyond the front lawn was a large building that looked like a four-layer vanilla cake. Its windows were a frosted white so you couldn't see inside.

The ornament on the gate was a friendly-looking gargoyle. As kids passed him, they touched his head. Maybe it was for good luck, so as I entered, I tapped his head too.

"Are you Winnie Burton?" I turned to see a girl about my age, but a little shorter and heavier than me.

Alarm bells went off in my head, and I instantly went into full-armor mode. When we'd been on the run from Granddad Jarvis, his detectives even hired kids and teachers to check out new transfer students. I'd learned to suspect anyone who was too friendly or curious.

"How do you know my name?" I demanded.

She leaned her head back, surprised by my frown. "I'm Mabli Whitlock. My aunt is your mother's lawyer. She said you might need to see a friendly face."

Miss Drake had said our lawyer was a dwarf, though she'd worn a human shape when she had met with Mom and me. That meant Mabli was a dwarf too and probably okay.

But Mom and I hadn't stayed free by being careless.

"Thanks, but you don't have to hang out with me," I said as I walked through the gates.

"Nervous?" she asked as she fell into step beside me.

"Some," I said cautiously.

After we stepped inside the school, Mabli took a leather rectangle from her pocket. At first, I thought it held her bus pass, but I saw a strange design on it.

"What's that?" I asked.

"It's a charm that lets me take human shape," Mabli said. "All the magical kids use something like this." She took a small case from her backpack and slipped the charm inside. "The case's material blocks the spell." When she zipped it up, she didn't grow shorter, but her shoulders broadened and her arms and legs thickened like a linebacker's. "What room are you?"

I ignored her as I started to walk along the hallway, looking for my locker.

Miss Drake had told me elementary classes were on the first floor, so I assumed my locker was too. Middle schoolers were on the second floor and high schoolers on the third, so schoolgirls were heading up one of the three staircases—left, right, and center.

As I walked, I saw what I thought were human girls, but there were also students with horns, feathers, and scales, of all sizes and shapes. Miss Drake had said if humans could come to San Francisco from around the world, why couldn't magical creatures too?

I figured that maybe two or three out of every five kids

looked like magicals. The only thing we had in common was our uniform.

Mabli stayed with me.

"Are you following me?" I asked suspiciously.

Annoyed, Mabli pointed down the hall. "My locker's 153, so it's this way."

Mine was 149. I began to feel a little guilty.

Stopping, I took my phone from my pocket and texted Miss Drake.

U no Dylis niece Mabli? She @ Spriggs?

A few minutes later, I read:

Yes, Mabli your age. Goes 2 Spriggs.

I went over to Mabli's locker. "I guess I was rude."

She glanced at me sideways. "You guessed right."

I wasn't used to apologizing. "It's just that Spriggs is"—I nodded my head from side to side to indicate the building and the students—"so much to handle."

"Is this your first time with magicals?" Mabli asked. "At least that you know about?"

"I've never met magicals my age." I added with a grin, "At least that I know about."

Mabli smiled back. "I was scared when I met my first naturals after all the stories I'd heard."

"Stories about what?" I asked, curious.

She took out our English textbook. "Mobs with torches and pitchforks."

"We do that only if they cancel the World Series," I said. "Is your first class in 104 too?"

"Yeah, we must be together," she said. "So if you've got questions, feel free to ask."

"Anyone I should watch out for?" I asked.

I think Mabli had been expecting a more practical question like *Where are the restrooms?* but she said in a low voice, "Just steer clear of Nanette, and you'll be fine." She nodded to a blond girl our age about fifty feet ahead of us, showing her new tablet to some other students. "She belongs to the Voisin clan. A lot of them are powerful magicians and sorceresses."

I'd met Nanette's aunt Silana at the Enchanters' Fair last summer. I hoped Nanette was nothing like her.

Close by was a girl with short gray hair. "And that's Nanette's friend Lupe. Stay out of her way too," Mabli whispered. "Especially on nights with full moons."

I'd seen enough horror movies to put two and two together. "She's a werewolf?"

"That's what she tells everyone," Mabli said softly.

"But in gym glass, she's got this funny, stumpy run. I bet there's some dachshund blood that got mixed in somehow."

"Were-dachshund." I laughed out loud.

Mabli was too late shushing me. Lupe twisted her head around and stared at me. "Uh-oh," Mabli said. "I should have warned you that Lupe's got sharp ears."

I saw Lupe say something to Nanette, who turned to look at me too. She pressed her lips together in a tight smile. I knew what that meant. I'd seen it often enough. It was a bully's grin.

I groaned to myself. So much for my promise to Mom.

But as I reached the first floor, Winnie was still talking with her mother.

I had yet to decide if I could tell Liza the truth about me. She was curious, and so to distract her I'd set up the job at Rhiannon's stable.

As I listened to her say good-bye to Winnie, I couldn't help contrasting Liza's gentle manner with her father Jarvis's, who had all the delicacy of a bulldozer. With everything he had done to her, it was amazing she had grown up into such a sweet person.

With a last burst of speed, I landed on Winnie's backpack. She looked like a Sherpa carrying the gear to climb Mount Everest rather than a ten-year-old girl going to school.

When Winnie finally stepped outside, I saw Paradise. She waited until Winnie had passed by before she nodded to me. I knew that she had told all her friends nearby to be alert to anything troublesome. No harm would come to my pet.

So, as Winnie walked by the small gardens, I pointed my paw at her. The spirits in the trees and shrubs and flowers rustled their acknowledgment. Grasshoppers and butterflies flapped their wings in greeting.

Rivera, a robin from an old, outstanding family, arose and flew high overhead. When Amelia—or Fluffy, as I al-

CHAPTER TWO

Magical or natural, mineral or ethereal, we are all Spriggs-ians now and forever.

FROM THE STUDENT HANDBOOK OF THE SPRIGGS ACADEMY

∾ MISS DRAKE ∾

I stepped out of my apartment and locked the door. Then I traced an ever-tightening spiral in the air. The moment I wrote *parhāni*, I began to shrink.

The trouble was that now it took longer to travel the distance the normal-size me could cover.

ways called her—was young, she found Rivera's ancestor with a broken wing and nursed him to health. Rivera's family—and all the robins—had not forgotten the kindness. Fluffy's kin was their kin now.

With them to watch over Winnie, I was free to inspect the traffic. The street was busy with people dropping students off at the Academy, so all the vehicles moved slowly. That was when I saw the two men in the black SUV. One of them quickly raised a large camera and snapped a picture of Winnie. Then he hurriedly dropped the camera out of sight.

I waved to Rivera, and with a dip of his wings, he drifted over the SUV, ready to follow to wherever they were staying.

I'd used magic to adapt my regular phone so that it could shrink and expand with me. So I slipped it from a special pouch behind a scale on my leg armor and took a photo of the license. Then I sent it to Reynard.

I noticed a tumbler pigeon above me, waiting for my next commands. I recognized Pietro, whose family lived among the steeples of Saints Peter and Paul's in the North Beach district. Years ago, I'd helped them escape a gang of crows. The family always repaid their debts. It gave me a warm feeling to know that the word had spread beyond my neighborhood to my friends throughout the city. Jarvis's thugs couldn't sneeze without my knowing it.

Once we reached the Academy gates, I knew Winnie would be safe. Though the metal fences looked plain, I could see faint but intricate tracings etched on them that were more than decorations. They were powerful wards against spells. And the gargoyles ringing the fence and roof guarded against physical intrusions.

Even without all of its security measures, no magical would burglarize the school. Everyone wanted a safe place where their young could learn. When fighting broke out between magical clans, the school and its students were always left alone. Everyone knew that if they harmed either one, the other clans would crush them.

When I saw that Dylis's niece, Mabli, had met Winnie, I knew my pet was in good hands. I'd met Mabli a few times at family dinners. Even when she was young, Mabli was as kind and conscientious as her aunt.

So I flew up to the gardens on the rooftop, where I had arranged to meet the principal, Ms. Griffin. She'd been very gracious when I'd called last night to warn about the danger to Winnie.

Ms. Griffin was a short woman whose black hair framed her face in a circle of tight ringlets. Intertwined among the curls were small gold beads shaped like pinecones and buckets. Her business suit was of a simple cut and dark navy blue, but the cuffs were edged with wavy lines of shiny thread and silver fish—as if she had streams of water encircling her wrists.

She came from a long line of respected African American educators, but the symbols in her hair and on her cuffs suggested she could trace her roots back to the sages of ancient Babylon. And several of her guardian gargoyles could have graced Babylonian temples— which was fitting since Spriggs was a temple of learning.

When I'd grown to my normal size again, I shook her hand. "Thank you for being so understanding, Ms. Griffin. I know how busy you are this morning."

She smiled. "Winnie is one of ours now. I've explained the situation to the staff, so they'll be keeping an eye on her."

I knew the staff was more than the teachers and maintenance people but the school gargoyles as well. "Thank you. If you don't mind, I'll stay with Winnie today to see how she's adjusting, but after this, I'll just escort her to and from home."

She waved a hand as if thanks were not necessary. "Winnie's a Spriggs-ian now. Nothing will happen to her here." Then she pointed at a small shed on the roof. "That covers the stairway that will take us into the school. There is an electronic lock on the doorway plus a magical ward," she added. "Winnie will probably be at her locker on the first floor. That would be locker 149."

Before me was the light well at the center of the flights of stairs. I had not heard such a volume of noise since Fluffy had graduated. It swelled up and around me now like a whirlpool: lockers slamming, shoes squeaking on freshly waxed floors, and, above all, the voices of the new and returning students. Their words were indistinguishable, so the sound was raw happiness, excitement, relief, and nervous anticipation. It was everything that intrigued me about naturals.

And so I darted down, down the light well. The music, visual arts, science, and magic classrooms were all on the top floor for all the grades. As I flew past, I saw some students already waiting for the doors to open. They were wearing uniforms very similar to the ones Fluffy had worn.

These early birds were the opposite of Fluffy, who was often late. It wasn't intentional. She was such a friendly soul that she often paused to chat and then had to make a mad dash for her class. Her shoes would slap the steps in a frantic rhythm, hair flying and books on the verge of falling from her arms.

Small statues of gargoyles were posted along the banisters or on the molding along the walls. Like their kin on the fences, they protected the school and the students. I felt the gargoyles' eyes follow my descent.

A photograph of an elderly Fluffy hung in pride of place next to the trophy case on the first floor. Fluffy had been generous with her time and money to her alma mater, endowing several scholarships for students who could not afford the tuition.

If you had a powerful magnifying glass, you could see me perched proudly on her shoulder next to the pearl necklace I had given her. Fluffy had insisted I pose with her.

I was lost in my memories when I felt my phone vibrate. It was a text from Winnie asking about Dylis's niece, and I texted her back to calm her fears.

It was odd for a hatchling her age to be so suspicious— her great-aunt Fluffy had been the opposite, almost too trusting for her own good.

When I found Winnie, she was standing with her back to the wall as if she expected to be attacked by the students surrounding her. But all Mabli was doing was introducing her to some of the other hatchlings.

"And this is Liri." Mabli motioned to a tall girl with short green hair. From the way her silvery-white skin rippled, I guessed she was a naiad whose family had once lived in some spring. As San Francisco had expanded, it had filled in its ponds and streams to build houses over them. But the water was still there if a naiad family dug a well deep enough for all the comforts of a damp home with cable and Wi-Fi.

"Hi, where are you from?" Liri asked, holding out her hand. "I've lived lots of places." Winnie barely touched her fingertips against Liri's before she snatched her hand back.

The other girls waited for Winnie to name some of the cities where she had been, but Winnie just stared at them.

Mabli filled in the awkward silence by nodding to another girl. "And this is Zaina. She's a djinn. Her family flew here from Morocco long before there were airplanes."

"Hello," Zaina said. Her eyes were a glowing amber with fiery red pupils, and her skin changed color constantly with swirls of yellow and tan like sand dancing in the wind. Occasionally, the sand thinned enough so that I could see how her flaming blood pulsed through a burning lace of arteries and veins.

Winnie still said nothing. At home, it was impossible to get Winnie to *stop* talking, so I didn't understand why she was so stingy with her words now. Couldn't she see there was all this good will waiting to be tapped?

At that moment, two hatchlings passed. Though the pepper-haired one looked human enough, she had the scent of wolf to her.

The other was blond, and her school uniform looked tailored just for her. I recognized her as Nanette Cellini, the niece of the sorceress and my self-proclaimed rival, Silana Voisin.

"They're letting in all sorts of trash nowadays on scholarship, aren't they, Lupe?" Nanette sneered. Apparently, the girl had inherited her aunt's genes for nastiness.

Winnie took a step toward her but stopped abruptly and simply glared. I knew that if there were a fight, the bat-headed gargoyle decorating an office doorway would not interfere. She was there to stop invaders, not referee fights between students.

It was Mabli who pointed toward Fluffy's photograph. "That's Winnie's great-aunt up there. I don't see your family's picture anywhere, Nanette."

If Mabli thought this would humble Nanette, she was wrong. "Oh, so Winnie's the trailer trash that inherited the Granger mansion. My father says they lowered the property values when they moved in."

I was tempted to set her straight: any property with dragons tripled in value, but I was worried about Winnie.

When you have brought up as many pets as I have, you

learn to read the nonverbal signs of aggression. Everything about Winnie's body screamed she was ready to attack. She stood stiff as a spear shaft, and her free hand opened and closed into a fist. Even the muscles around Winnie's jaw worked as if she were swallowing angry retorts.

Yet she said and did nothing. I was surprised at her self-control. My training was bearing fruit—oh, all right, and maybe her mother's advice had reinforced my training.

I confess that I was tempted to take a nip out of Nanette, but I refrained. I didn't have anything to wash her nasty taste from my mouth.

Suddenly a tall girl with dark skin and a wild mane of red hair grabbed Nanette by the shoulder and spun her around. "What's wrong with scholarship students?"

Lupe turned sideways, trying to keep an eye on the redhead as well as Winnie. "Stay out of this, Saskia."

"Nanette made it my business by insulting me," Saskia said. There was the faintest scent of horse to her—likely some centaur blood ran in her family. Centaurs are reputed to be wise when they're old, but they can be reckless when they're hatchlings. This one combined the spirit of a wild filly with the hotheadedness of a young natural, a dangerous recipe in anyone's book.

Lupe eyed her warily. Werewolf cubs wrestle one another for fun as well as practice for establishing a place in the pack. By now, Lupe was probably good at judging her opponent's abilities. She obviously didn't like her chances of winning. "Can't you take a joke?"

"No," Saskia said flatly.

"Oh, just leave these losers, Lupe," Nanette said, walking away. I knew her type now. She was one of those rich girls who expected someone else to clean up the messes that they made.

Lupe glowered at Saskia as if to warn her not to interfere in their games next time, and then she hurried after her friend.

"Uh, thanks," Winnie said.

"I did it as a thank-you to your great-aunt. I wouldn't be here without one of the scholarships she set up." Saskia added scornfully, "I didn't do it to help a rich brat like you."

Winnie bristled. "I'm not—" She stopped herself before she said she was poor, because that was no longer true, thanks to Fluffy. "I'm not a brat. And next time, don't bother. I can take care of myself."

"No, you can't," Saskia said, again in that flat, defiant tone. I sensed she was one of those people who made judgments quickly and then rarely changed them—as if they were carved in stone. "But suit yourself."

Winnie nodded at Saskia as she strolled away. "What's her story, anyway?"

When Liri shrugged, her shoulders rippled under her uniform. "Her grandmother was once the chief of the centaurs. It's in Saskia's blood to be the alpha in the herd."

Just as it was in the blood of my rival's niece to dislike my pet.

....

∽ Winnie ∽

As we walked into 104, our homeroom, I couldn't help wondering if there was something wrong with me. Why did I rub some people the wrong way?

But as we passed by the teacher's desk, I noticed the stacks of yellow hard hats. Each of them had the school crest.

"Why do we need hard hats for English class?" I asked Mabli.

"I hear our teacher, Ms. Kululu, likes to surprise her classes," Mabli said. She was going to sit in the nearest seat, which happened to be in the front, right by the door. Well, there's something to be said for getting out of a classroom as quickly as you can.

I looked around to get the lay of the room. Nanette and Lupe were sitting in desks by the windows, so I knew I wasn't going there. Liri and Saskia were in the back, and there were two empty desks behind them.

I nudged Mabli. "Let's go there."

"I won't be able to see the board," Mabli protested.

"You've got ears. You'll be able to hear the lesson," I pointed out. "And this way we can hide. The teacher can't pick on students she can't see."

Mabli drew her eyebrows together. "What kind of school did you go to before?"

"Schools," I said. "Lots of them and I learned to keep my head low."

Mabli folded her arms. "Well, if you haven't noticed, my head's already pretty low. So this is where I need and want to be." For a moment, she reminded me of a boulder cemented to the desk. It was my first taste of dwarf stubbornness, but not my last.

"Suit yourself," I said. I'd given her a chance. Let her sit in front of the bull's-eye.

I'd gone maybe two yards down the aisle when something bit my neck. It felt like a pesky mosquito, so I slapped the spot. I hadn't taken more than another step, when I heard a loud, high humming sound and then the door closed.

"Take a seat, miss," a voice said.

I turned to see a two-foot-high bird-woman hovering behind the teacher's desk. Her dark eyes gazed at me, her foot-long beak poking the air like a fencing sword. Instead of hair, she had blue-green feathers that rose into a crest. She wore a ruby-red vest, and her beating wings blurred. She wore a pair of tan slacks but no shoes, for instead of feet, she had delicate claws. Her right claw held a pouch of bags, and her left claw was pointing to the empty desk by Mabli.

So much for trying to stay invisible to the teacher. I immediately took the seat by Mabli, who gave me a friendly nod.

Nervous, I put my hands into my sweater pocket and found a small package of trail mix. Mom had attached a note to it: *To keep up your strength.*

Good old Mom. That made me feel better.

The teacher set her pouch down on top of her desk. Then she pirouetted gracefully through the air to the board behind her. Because it was slick and black, I had assumed it was the usual chalkboard. Instead, her claw began to write her name across it in pink glowing letters:

"Good morning, class," she said in a flutelike voice. "I am Ms. Kululu, your homeroom and English teacher. Spriggs prides itself on helping you become a well-rounded individual. You will learn the basics and also have a knowledge of music, the visual arts, and magic."

To pack in the courses, we would be at Spriggs from 9 a.m. to 4:30 p.m. every day.

After she had taken roll call, she darted higher and flew over the desk with the hard hats and then down the aisle next to me.

"Because you already speak English, you think you know everything about it. But during this year, I will show you how words can lighten your hearts and make your minds fly where you want," she said enthusiastically as she passed. The breeze from her beating wings brushed my cheek. She smelled like fresh-cut grass on a summer afternoon.

Ms. Kululu spun in a slow circle, her wings whirring. "On our first day, I like to have some fun with the summer reading list. But this will also test your memory and comprehension."

I couldn't help groaning. But then so did a lot of other

girls. "A test on the first day?" I muttered to myself. "That's not fair."

I swear I could almost hear Miss Drake whispering to me, "Of course not. Life isn't fair."

But then Ms. Kululu told the students in front to get a stack of hard hats and pass them out. This was another reason I didn't like to sit here. The teacher always "volunteered" you for chores.

As Mabli and I walked to Ms. Kululu's desk, I whispered, "Are we going to build something?"

"Your guess is as good as mine," she murmured back. She took a hat from the top of a stack and set it on her head. The hats came with chin straps, and she pulled the elastic under her jaw.

When everyone had a hat, Ms. Kululu darted here and there helping students. She had to use some magic to make one fit Lena, who had a pair of horns curling against her head.

Then she flew back to her desk and took a batch of blank paper from her pouch. "I've cast a spell over these. Please write your answers on them."

Again, the girls in front had to pass out the sheets. When we were finished, Ms. Kululu said, "The poetry collection you read this summer has some of my favorite poems. So right now I'm going to recite lines from a poem. Please write down the name of the poet who wrote it."

I'd found out I was going to Spriggs a few weeks ago, so I'd barely finished the reading. Even then, I'd skimmed a lot. I knew I was in trouble.

"What genius penned this noble sentiment?" Ms. Kululu asked and then recited:

> *"For with a lark's heart he doth tower,*
> *By a glorious upward instinct drawn."*

I guessed and wrote down *Shakespeare* and heard a little groan from someone.

"The next one is harder," Ms. Kululu said, "because the poet based it on a very old style of poetry. We'll study it in detail later." Lifting her beak, she said,

> *"High there, how he rung upon the rein of a*
> *   wimpling wing*
> *In his ecstasy! then off, off forth on swing."*

I couldn't think of a name, so I put down *the same writer who did the song "The Man on the Flying Trapeze."*

This time I felt something small and hard poke me

between the shoulder blades. If it was a bug, it was an odd sort of one.

"And finally," Ms. Kululu said, "who wrote these immortal lines?"

"Oh! I have slipped the surly bonds of Earth
And danced the skies on laughter-silvered
wings."

At that point, I just gave up and scribbled *Rudolph the Red-Nosed Reindeer.*

When the bug bit me again, I got mad, slapping the spot to put it and me out of my misery.

Ms. Kululu gave us time to finish, then looked around. "Everybody done?" She paused and said, "Please hold on tight to your answer sheet while I tell you the correct names of the poets."

There were a lot of rustlings as we picked up our papers, but everyone looked puzzled.

"There won't be any grades for this test—it's just for fun," Ms. Kululu explained. "The first poet was James Russell Lowell, and the poem was 'The Falcon.' "

"What?" Mabli said in surprise.

I turned to see her floating off her seat. Her knees

bumped the underside of her desk. From the thumping behind me, I guessed others were gravity-free too.

Carefully, Mabli swung her legs into the aisle and drifted up a couple of feet. About half my classmates were now sitting or standing above their desks.

"Wonderful," Ms. Kululu said. "Didn't I tell you words would lighten your hearts? Each correct answer will take you higher."

I loved flying with Miss Drake, but I'd never flown on my own. I was jealous as Mabli spun like a ballerina.

"Get ready," Ms. Kululu warned the floaters. "The next poem was by Gerard Manley Hopkins from 'The Windhover.'"

"Wow!" Mabli cried happily as she shot more than a yard straight up in the air. I looked about and saw nine other girls had gained the same height.

"Fabulous. Now be prepared to soar," Ms. Kululu encouraged them. "And the third poet was John Gillespie Magee Jr., who wrote 'High Flight' before he died all too soon."

The next moment, I saw the reason for the hard hats, when Mabli shot upward so fast she bumped against the ceiling. Saskia's hat slapped the plaster at the same time, and they both began to laugh.

"Outstanding! You've *rizzen* to the occazion." Ms. Kululu zipped upward and began to circle overhead, gesturing to Mabli and Saskia to join her. I guess when she got excited, she spoke her *s*'s more like *z*'s.

My teacher grabbed my classmates' hands, and grinning like mad, they began to dance over my head.

The other girls at the lower heights began to enjoy themselves as well. Zaina had gotten only one question right, so she stared longingly above her. As she started to rise, Ms. Kululu called to her, "No cheating, Zaina. Stay where you are."

I guess Zaina, being mostly wind and sand inside, was very light. She settled down to her old level and began to move about with a butterfly stroke.

A damp hand patted my head. I looked up at Liri darting over me. "Let's play tag, Winnie. You're it."

Part of me wanted to do just that.

But another part of me warned, *Don't be stupid, Winnie. This is how bullies have set you up before. They draw you into a game and then make you the goat.*

I started to shake my head, when something nipped my behind hard. "Ow," I said. I scrambled out of my desk so fast that I bumped Liri's chin.

For a fancy school, Spriggs had an awful lot of mosquitoes and fleas. They needed an exterminator big-time.

Liri had drifted a foot higher as she rubbed her jaw. Her whole face wobbled like a water balloon.

Usually, when I hit someone, it's because I mean to. "Sorry. Are you okay?"

She smiled. "I guess I'm it."

This friendship thing with Liri was happening way too quickly, but suddenly I didn't care. I just wanted to have fun.

Pivoting, I started to run down the aisle. I saw Liri was kicking her legs as if she were swimming. Flying was still new to her, but she was picking it up swiftly.

Just as she was about to reach me, I put a hand on a desktop and pushed off at the same time I jumped. Landing on the seat, I hopped into the next aisle.

Liri was good on a straight flight path, but she was having trouble with her turns.

"You look like an old tugboat," I teased.

Liri beat her arms at the air, slowly pulling herself around. "Just wait until I catch you."

"Says you," I said, and started to run, ducking under the kicking feet of a girl who flew by. That was when I saw Nanette still at her desk. She was the only other zero girl. She frowned as if she had just realized the same thing.

Okay, new school, new start, new *me*. I'd try again to

get off to a better start with her. So I gave Nanette a little grin and invited her: "We can still play tag even if we're both grounded."

"We will *never* be down on the same level." Nanette's every word dripped icicles. Then she looked out the window as she pretended to be bored.

I'd met snooty girls like Nanette before. The best thing to do was to ignore them.

....

⌒ MISS DRAKE ⌒

I am a firm believer that pets should be pets, so no cute costumes, no adorable tricks, and, above all, no muzzles for my little friends. On the other hand, Winnie's bad behavior would reflect upon me. So when she tried to sneak into the back of the classroom or wrote funny answers on her tests, I'd given her little disciplinary nips.

But it was my fault she did so poorly on her poetry test. I had been enjoying our adventures together so much that I had neglected her studies. After this episode, I would have to manage our time better, and for my penance tonight, I would forgo my evening snack of *taiyaki* pastries that I'd gotten from Clipper's Traveling

Emporium. I loved the fish-shaped cakes, and these had a special filling of seaweed and lobster cream, but sacrifices must be made and good character maintained.

After all, how can one be firm with one's pet if one cannot be firm with oneself?

CHAPTER THREE

A Spriggs-ian should be able to count to ten on her fingers
or claws, paint a bowl of fruit, and protect herself from
unwanted spells and monsters.

FROM THE STUDENT HANDBOOK OF THE SPRIGGS ACADEMY

Winnie

Our next period was magic. I was so excited I wanted to take the stairs two steps at a time, but Mabli couldn't have kept up. I'd been trying to get Miss Drake to give me magic lessons. I wanted to grow big, then shrink and change shapes like she did. But she claimed she wasn't qualified to teach me—though she was so stuffed with magic it practically dripped from every claw.

That's the drawback to having a dragon: you can't make one do anything she doesn't want to do. Even if I could send her to an obedience school, she'd just burn it down.

When I entered room 411 for my first magic lesson, I thought there'd be cages of bats hanging from the ceiling and shrunken heads and a broomstick or two. But it was a real letdown, just a regular classroom with desks, a bulletin board with a map (though it was of Atlantis, not of America), and an autographed photo of Merlin. Was that some kind of joke?

The planter boxes near the windows were just as disappointing. I drifted over there, expecting to see something weird, like meat-eating plants. Then I read the little signs on stakes: *garlic, rosemary,* and *thyme.* Vasilisa could have used any of them when she cooked. The most exotic one was mugwort, and that sounded more like an insult than a plant.

In the front was a counter with a sink, and behind them was a blackboard. On it, someone had written in large glowing letters:

Lady Louhi

Also on the board was our first homework assignment with a box drawn around it. We were to read chapter four, "Cryptid Fun," in our textbook, *Magic, the World, and Us.*

At least the rear wall looked like it belonged in a magic classroom. I thought it was a giant sheet of metal and someone had etched a forest on it. Then I noticed that the trees were swaying.

My other classmates were staring at it. Nanette had folded her arms and complained to Lupe. "I don't know what a tree hugger can teach us about magic."

"Tree hugger?" I whispered to Zaina.

"It's what sorceresses call witches, because they do a lot of magic outdoors and use a lot of herbs and natural ingredients," Zaina explained.

"And what do witches call sorceresses?" I wondered.

Nanette heard me even though I spoke in a low voice. "Sketchies . . . because we draw so many diagrams and symbols. But naturals like you better not call us that."

"Ease up, Nanette," I said as I reached out my hand to touch the wall. It rippled around my fingertips, then my arm went through it. Inside—or was it beyond?—I felt cool, misty air.

I snatched my hand back, but my skin was still dry. The next moment, I heard a drumming sound from the tree in front of me. I reached into the wall again and drew back a small branch.

Behind it, on a large branch, was a red squirrel wearing a tiny derby between his tall, triangle-shaped ears. He was beating the bark with a stick like someone tapping out a code. He stopped when he saw me and lifted his derby as a hello.

In the distance, I heard a woman say, "Oh dear, oh dear, oh dear. Is it that time already? Coming, coming."

The squirrel looked so cute I wanted to do something nice for him. So I took the package of trail mix from my pocket. "Want some?" I cooed, and tore it open with my teeth.

He leaped into the classroom toward me, turned his hat upside down, and held it out for me to fill. But I heard the rhythmic beating of hooves coming real quick. I knew animals, and I knew when one was galloping.

"Something's coming," I yelled to the others. "Get away from the wall."

A heartbeat later, a very large reindeer burst into the classroom, broad hooves stomping and skidding over the floorboards. It just brushed me, but it was so huge it was like being bumped by a car. I would have fallen over, but the rider grabbed me by the wrist and pulled me up.

Thanks to my warning, my classmates had time to

back up. The reindeer swerved to the right, trying not to collide with anyone else, and began to circle. Because the rider held my wrist in an iron grip, I swung through the air like a worm on a fishing hook.

The classroom whirled round and round. I didn't want to get dizzy, so I kept my eyes on the saddle, bridle, and reins. The riding tack was elegant—red leather with designs in gold wire.

The rider was a plump woman, her long pearly-gray cape flying behind her. She'd woven her long blond hair into two braids that were coiled on top of her head, but the pins went flying, so her braids were whipping all about. I thought her light blue felt blouse and green trousers had strange brown mystical signs on them. But then I saw that the lid from her Halloween commuter mug had come off, and the coffee was spattering her clothes, the reindeer, and me.

I know horses that would have gotten spooked by being suddenly surrounded by a lot of screaming, frightened girls. And I know more riders who would have gotten thrown out of the saddle by a mount twisting so violently. But neither the reindeer nor the woman panicked.

They managed to stop without hitting anyone else, and she lowered me until my feet touched the floor again.

"Are you all right, dear?" she asked.

Before I could tell her that I felt a little dizzy, some-thing tugged at my sock. When I looked down, I saw the red squirrel. He held out his derby hat in both paws.

The woman clicked her tongue. "The squirrels are getting shameless, and Sassafras is the most shameless of all. None of the animals in my forest go hungry, but they just love human snacks. They'd pester all my classes if I let them." She pointed to the wall. "You know the rules, Sassafras. No begging."

"Excuse me," I said, holding up the empty package. The trail mix itself was scattered all around the floor. "I'm the one who offered food to him first."

The woman dipped her head. "I apologize, Sassafras. You may take what you can carry in your hat, but no more than that."

The squirrel gave a tiny sniff and, lifting his tail in a dignified way, began to gather up sunflower seeds, raisins, and nuts and put them into his hat.

Dismounting, the woman patted the reindeer on his hip. "Thank you, Emil." As he and Sassafras walked back through the wall, she nodded to me. "What's your name, dear?"

"Winnie Burton," I said.

"Well, Winnie Burton, I am your magic teacher, Lady

Louhi." She used her free hand to shoo us toward the desks. "Please sit down, ladies, and I'll take your names."

Nanette and Lupe settled again by the window. Mabli sat in front, so I joined her.

Lady Louhi hung her cape up on a hook, took a tablet from a pouch on her cloth belt, and began recording our names and seats. When she finished, she took out a five-pound bag of potting soil from behind the counter and set it on top. "In your other classes, you learn about the languages, histories, and cultures of the many types of naturals. In my class, you'll learn about the languages, histories, and cultures of the many types of magicals."

Then she took out a big glass bowl and pitcher. "But first of all, I want to make it clear that the only one who will cast spells in here is me."

I couldn't hide my disappointment. Putting up my hand, I asked, "You mean you're not going to teach us how to do magic?"

The class started to laugh but stopped when Lady Louhi held up a hand. "We do not make fun of one another. The only silly question is the one that goes unasked." Then she said gently to me, "No, my dear. You're going to learn the history and culture of the different magical clans—though occasionally, like today, I'll perform an enchantment to illustrate a point. Actual spell casting is an after-school elective and only if you can demonstrate potential.

"But that leads me to my first question." Lady Louhi filled the pitcher with water. "Do only magicals have magic?"

A girl with black hair named Kari Wong—I think she was a human like me—finally said, "Every living creature has a little magic whether they're naturals or magicals."

"Just as every living being carries a teeny electrical charge." Lady Louhi poured soil from the bag into the bowl. "Magicals happen to have more magic in them because that's what lets them fly or change shape. But does that mean every magical can cast an enchantment?"

Mabli put up her hand and said, "I'm a magical, and I can't transform myself. I had to buy a charm to do that."

Miss Drake made enchantments look so easy to do, but I was beginning to realize that was because she was so good at it.

"Exactly," Lady Louhi said. "Even though magicals are full of magic, most of them can't do a spell any more than a natural can. They have to buy charms like everyone else."

She dipped a finger into the pitcher of water and wrote something on the countertop that I couldn't see. "Here are three important things to keep in mind about magic. The first is that magic cannot make something from nothing." Then she lowered her head so we couldn't see her lips. She didn't so much whisper the spell as sing it, because, as I learned later, she came from a line of northern witches who used a singing magic.

Since Lady Louhi kept her hands behind the counter, I couldn't see what gestures she made either. Then she raised her hand with the palm up. A packet of something appeared in her hand the next moment.

"Now, it seems as if this came out of thin air." She dangled the package between a thumb and index finger so we could see it was full of seeds. "But in fact, what I did was draw from the elements around me to make this."

Tearing open the packet, she poked one of the seeds deep into the dirt of the glass bowl. With more water from the pitcher, she wrote something unseen on the bowl's side.

Suddenly a marigold sprouted from the dirt and kept growing until it was almost two feet high. "Second, magic is not abnormal. Often, it merely speeds up, slows down, or stops everyday processes. Magic complements the ordinary by being extraordinary."

She stepped away from the counter. "And what do

you think the third thing is? I'll give you a hint. It's the greatest force in the universe."

Nanette's hand shot up. "Magic is more powerful than anything else."

Lady Louhi smiled as she shook her head. "Students make the mistake of assuming that magic will solve everything."

Nanette refused to back down. "But my aunt is Silana Voisin, the mightiest sorceress, and she says—"

Lady Louhi cut her off with a friendly nod. "I'm well aware who your aunt is, Nanette, and with all due respect to her, magic often complicates a problem rather than fixing it."

"Witches might use that as an excuse to give up," Nanette said contemptuously. "But a sorceress will keep trying spells until she fixes the problem. If you're only a natural, you better buy charms from a sorceress rather than a witch."

Despite the open challenge, Lady Louhi kept her temper. "Nanette, do you know what the difference is between witches and sorceresses?"

Nanette must have sensed she'd gone too far because she said simply, "No. What?"

"Witchery and sorcery overlap on many things," Lady Louhi explained. "The main difference is attitude.

Witches act like little sisters who coax Mother Nature into doing what She needs to do. Sorceresses are like bossy big sisters who tell Mother Nature what they *want* Her to do."

When the class finished laughing, Lady Louhi went on. "What I have in mind is a force both naturals and magicals have that works even without spells or charms."

Dad had been big on riddles. It was almost like debating with him again. When I thought I had the answer, I started to raise my hand but lowered it because I didn't want anyone to laugh at me.

Lady Louhi, though, saw me. "Yes, Winnie?"

"Is it . . . your brain?" I asked.

Lady Louhi nodded. "Yes. In the end, it's what makes all naturals and magicals equal."

I settled back in my seat, satisfied. But I saw Nanette frowning at me.

Well, excuse me for breathing the same air as you.

....

∾ MISS DRAKE ∾

Like her aunt Silana, Nanette's mind was an open book, and most of the pages were unpleasant to read. For the rest of magic class, whenever she glanced at Winnie, it was with a sour look. Had her aunt Silana told her to pick on Winnie? Was Silana trying to strike at me by striking at my pet?

....

⤨ Winnie ⤪

The next period was science. The lab itself was what I expected. There was a big counter at the front with a long sink, and then rows of tables and stools.

At a fancy school like this, I thought the science teacher would be in a lab coat. I didn't expect him to be wearing a long, curly brown wig on his head, a frilly white shirt, and maroon pants that only came down to his calves. A blue velvet coat with gold brocade hung from a rack in the corner—on the coat was a black patch with crossed shinbones.

As we entered, he was writing his name on the board:

SIR ISAAC NEWTON

I didn't know much about history, but I'd seen a cartoon once. Newton was a scientist who discovered gravity when he watched an apple fall from a tree. But that was long, long ago.

I couldn't help going up to him. "Excuse me, Mr. Newton?"

"Sir Isaac, if you please." He underlined the first two words on the board for emphasis.

There's no polite way to ask someone this question, so I just plowed ahead. "Well . . . um . . . sorry, Sir Isaac, but aren't you sort of . . . dead?"

He whipped around, jerking abruptly. His bright blue eyes stared down his long nose at me. "I find it convenient to have most people think so, but let me assure you that I am quite corporeal." He poked a finger against my wrist. "Does that feel like ectoplasm to you?"

Well, his touch seemed real enough. "But how . . . ?"

"It's one of the side benefits of finding the philosopher's stone." Sir Isaac sighed when he saw my blank look. "Oh dear, I can see your head is emptier than most."

"Hey," I protested.

He smiled. "Do you want to nurse a false and foolish pride with an insincere apology from me, or do you wish to learn, Miss— What the deuce is your name anyway?"

I wish I could have given him a fake name, but I knew better than to risk it. "Winnie Burton."

"Well, Burton," he explained, "the philosopher's stone will let you change lead into gold."

I gasped. "Then everybody would be rich," I said.

"Perhaps you're not so foolish after all." Sir Isaac wasn't being sarcastic. He spoke in a flat tone as if he were telling me the sky was blue. "Now, Burton, keep in mind that in the past every nation's money was based on how valuable gold was because it was so rare. What would happen if gold became as common as . . . well . . . lead?"

I scratched my forehead. Sir Isaac was making my head ache. "If gold weren't valuable, then neither would silver or any other kind of money."

"Thus, the world would slip into chaos, hunger, and war. Q.E.D." He spread his arms wide as if hugging an explosion and then dropped his arms to his sides. "So if you were the smartest person in the world, what would you do instead?"

"Uh . . . I guess I wouldn't tell anyone that I'd found the philosopher's stone so things could go on the way they were," I said.

"That's exactly why I hid my greatest discovery from the world," he said.

"Okay, but what's that got to do with your not being dead yet?" I asked.

"The stone can also let me renew cells in my body, and no, do not ask me what cellular regeneration is. That must wait until your biology class in high school."

I may not have known what cellular regeneration was, but I could guess another reason he had kept the stone a secret. "Telling people you had a way to stay young would make even more trouble than telling them you could make gold, wouldn't it?"

His eyes twinkled. "Well done, Burton. I see my initial hypothesis about you was wrong."

"One more question?" I asked. "What's a *scientist* doing with a *philosopher's* stone?"

"Because what we once called natural philosophy is now termed science, so if anyone searched for it nowadays, we would call it the scientist's stone," Sir Isaac explained. "Now, the sooner you take a seat, the sooner I can begin pouring knowledge into the empty heads of your fellow students." And with a fingertip he began to write the glowing letters on the board:

GRAVITY

The other students ignored the fact that their teacher was a man from centuries ago. It made me wonder who

60

else was on the faculty as my classmates chose stools by one of the lab tables.

Mabli sat up front again, so I slid in beside her. "Huh, gravity. I wonder where the apples are," she murmured.

"How did people stay on the ground before he discovered gravity anyway?" I teased.

Mabli just rolled her eyes. "Please."

When the bell rang for the period to begin, Sir Isaac picked up an oiled parchment bag. "Here I have four ounces of feathers." He held up a second bag. "And in this one I have four ounces of water. Which will fall the faster?" He nodded to me. "What say you, Burton?"

"Well, feathers are lighter," I said slowly, "so I guess the water would drop quicker."

The wrinkles around his eyes crinkled as he set the bags back down on the counter. "Let's put your hypothesis to the test, shall we?" He raised his palm upward. *"Surge!"*

"That means 'rise' in Latin," Mabli whispered to me. "Get up."

"Bene," Sir Isaac praised.

When we formed a circle around him, he reached over to the counter and picked up a small brass block with a lot of tubes and wires. "Now for the rest of the experiment to work, we must all be quiet as mice." He set a finger against his lips for emphasis and then placed the device on the floor. As he began to turn a small crank on the top, gears started to click and turn inside, tubes went from blue to white, and sparks began to arc over the instrument.

I gasped when a six-inch circle of the floor disappeared to the left of the device, and I was looking down at the leaves of a very old oak tree below me. Music rose from the hole, and there was the sound of laughter.

"More roasted peacock, Your Highness?" a man asked.

With his buckled shoe, Sir Isaac pushed the device across the floor, and as the hole moved, I saw other parts of the tree as if I were looking through a small window. I saw men in long wigs and embroidered coats and women in gigantic gowns sitting in chairs on a lush lawn.

He adjusted the hole until it was over a tall man in a long, curly dark wig that spilled past his shoulders and down his back. From what I could see, his coat was completely covered with lace and gold braid.

Then from the counter Sir Isaac took a laser range finder and beamed it through the hole. A moment later, he wrote on the board:

DISTANCE FROM US TO THE GROUND = 64.3405 FEET.

Sir Isaac handed me his smartphone—the clock set to stopwatch—and pointed to a button. "Start timing the descent from the moment the bag enters the hole," he whispered, "till the moment you hear the scream."

Smiling slyly, Sir Isaac knelt on the floor with the bag of water in his hand and nodded to me. My thumb immediately pressed the button.

At the same time, the bag dropped through the hole. Two seconds later, I heard the *ploosh!*

"What the deuce?" someone cried.

After I had stopped the watch, I couldn't help peeking. The tall man had jumped to his feet, all wet.

A woman below us said, "You are to be congratulated on organizing the weather so well, Charley. The rain comes in such tidy little bags."

"My Lady Castlemaine, this is a certain educated scoundrel's doing and none of mine," Charley growled, looking all around.

Sir Isaac reset the stopwatch and then, with a wink, gave his phone to me again. As the bag of feathers dropped through the hole, I started the timer again.

Two seconds later, the bag hit with a *floosh!* A cloud of chicken feathers settled on Charley's damp wig, turning it almost all white. Sir Isaac skipped around the hole. "Refuse to knight me, will you?" he whispered gleefully. "At least, Queen Annie had some sense."

Charley shook his fist at the treetop and roared, "I know you're hiding up there, Newton! You rogue! You . . . you poulterer!"

Sir Isaac touched a button on top of the block, and the hole itself disappeared and the brass block was sitting in the middle of the floorboards. Then he straightened up and bowed to the class. "And now you can tell your social studies teacher that you know what King Charles II sounds like when his picnic is ruined."

"Sir Isaac, won't what you just did get the Newton back then in trouble?" I asked.

"No, because at the time of the royal picnic, I was fifty miles away giving a lecture to a hundred distinguished clerics." His eyes twinkled. "Sometimes a solid alibi is as valuable to a scientist as the latest computer."

Sir Isaac had me write on the board how long it took for each bag to fall. I asked, "Did you make the hole with the philosopher's stone?"

"No, it's another of my discoveries." Sir Isaac cradled the brass block in his hands. The tubes on it were still glowing blue, and now and then a spark arced across it. "Modern scientists would call it a mini-wormhole that crosses through space and time. It's perfect for conducting demonstrations."

I had a feeling that what Sir Isaac called demonstrations, others would call practical jokes.

"Wouldn't it be easier to use magic to drop your bags?" Nanette asked.

"Ah, but what if you are like me and have no magical powers?" Sir Isaac held up the brass block. "What is the real value of this device?"

"Uh, it's scientific," Nanette said.

"Don't guess." Sir Isaac tapped his forehead. *"Cogite bene!"*

"Think well," Mabli automatically translated out loud for me.

When we didn't have a lot of money, we had to figure out how to use what we had. I'd gotten used to finding new angles for things. "Not everyone can do magic," I said, "but anyone can push a button. Your invention will open a window on other times and spaces for people who aren't magicians."

"Yes, yes." Sir Isaac rocked up and down on the soles of his feet.

"That was sort of my answer," Nanette complained. Even if she couldn't see the reason for devices like Sir Isaac's, she wanted to get a good grade by answering a question about it.

Sir Isaac curled his fingers as if urging her to take

a step. "Then extend the logic to the philosopher's stone."

"Uh . . . does it have a button too?" Nanette asked.

"Quit guessing, Cellini." He swung around and pointed at me. "What say you, Burton?"

Even though Nanette was glaring at me, I thought about it and said, "Not everyone can do a spell to change lead into gold. But the philosopher's stone"—I remembered Sir Isaac's other term—"what you also called the scientist's stone, well, anyone can touch lead to it and make it gold."

Sir Isaac spread his arms. "Thus, *science is magic for everyone.* Q.E.D." He rounded on the rest of the class. "And before you scoff, my dear young scholars, consider what would happen if a vile villain stole your books of spells, your wands, and your magical charms and marooned you on a desert island?" He pointed at his forehead. "You would still have your brains to build a raft and get home."

"Now you're sounding like Lady Louhi," Nanette complained.

"Of course! Because with everything that our graduates achieve in magic and science, English and math, all Spriggs-ians have one trait in common: they use their brains." With that quick, peculiar motion of his, Sir

Isaac whipped around, the movement making a laser pointer slide from his cuff into his hand. The next moment, a bright red dot appeared by each of the experiment's times. "And so your adventure in science begins with this data. Be they water or be they feathers, we see that an equal weight falls at an equal rate over an equal distance."

I had never thought of school as fun before, but then, I'd never before had a hummingbird, a witch, or a maybe-immortal for teachers.

Too bad, Nanette, I said to her silently. *I'm going to stick around here for a while.*

....

⌒ MISS DRAKE ⌒

As I left with Winnie, Sir Isaac nodded in my direction even though I was only a speck. I nodded back respectfully on the chance that he could see me.

I'd met Sir Isaac when he'd been a boy building clever little model windmills. I'd found him abrupt and a little rude and without a sense of humor, the way hobbyists sometimes are. But centuries later, when he instructed Fluffy, I found that he had not only mellowed and become a good teacher but had developed a dry wit. Perhaps it had taken him this long to mature, but I like to think the students at Spriggs had taught him as much as he had taught them.

I hoped Spriggs would do the same for Winnie.

CHAPTER FOUR

~∽~

Teach your pet to welcome friends and avoid enemies . . .
unless they won't avoid her.

∽ Winnie ∽

B etween flying, water-bombing kings, and avoiding
stampeding reindeer, I was already feeling worn-
out by lunchtime. As I stowed my books in my locker,
Mabli told me, "You're free to go
outside as long as you stay
on the school grounds."

The old on-the-run
Winnie would have found
somewhere to hide so
she could eat her lunch

on her own. But I was now the new-and-improved Win-nie. What kind of Winnie was that, though? I'd have to work on her—maybe starting now.

"Want to come with me?" I asked as I took out Vasi-lisa's lunch bag.

Mabli shook her head. "I don't feel like getting out my charm just so I can enjoy some sunshine. Most of the magicals usually eat in the cafeteria."

Okay, I'd been polite. Now I was free to find a tree outside and grab a quick nap after my meal, but I felt a little sorry for Mabli.

Miss Drake had told me the magicals found it safer if most humans didn't know about them. They had formed the Agreement to keep their existence secret. But the magicals I'd met so far weren't any different on the in-side than the humans I'd known—some good, some bad. And Mabli was a lot nicer to me than any kid had been on my first day at a new school.

I thought sadly of that tree as I said, "I'll go with you if I can eat my own lunch."

"Sure," Mabli said. "A lot of magicals have special tastes and diets, so they bring their meals." She added in a low voice, "Watch out for Liri when she has a live eel for lunch."

"But your face always becomes the nicest shade of green when I do," Liri said, coming up from behind.

"I prefer lunches that don't wriggle," Mabli said.

"Have you guys known each other for a long time?" I asked as we started to walk down the stairs to the basement.

"Since kindergarten," Liri said.

Mabli made a face. "Back then, it was teeny-tiny baby eels, clear as glass."

"You've learned to turn a lot more shades of green since then," Liri teased.

The cafeteria was a large room in the basement that also doubled as an auditorium. The floors were made of boards from the decks of ships stranded here during the gold rush. Just like their passengers, sailors decided to seek gold, deserting their ships for the California hills. The floor planks didn't always match in size and color, but a clever carpenter had joined them together wonderfully.

There was already a line of students waiting at the hot food counter and salad bar. The fold-up tables were all in place and were filling fast.

"You go ahead and get your lunches," I told Mabli and Liri. "I'll grab seats for us."

As I walked down the center aisle scanning the tables for open spots, I was alert enough to see a foot suddenly stick out in front of me. I'd learned the hard way to keep a wary eye for pranks, so I gave a little hop over it.

"Oops," Nanette said. "I didn't see you when I started to get up."

I had a dozen things to say to her, but I remembered Mom's warning to avoid fights.

What would Mom do? I asked myself, and so I just turned and kept walking.

I found three spaces together and sat down in the middle, putting paper napkins on either side to save the seats. Then I opened my lunch bag and took out a little plastic box with a cheese sandwich and an apple. When no one was watching, I set Vasilisa's doll within the bag.

I tore up my sandwich and left part by her. "Small Doll, Small Doll, you must be hungry," I said softly. Then I set the lid of the box into the bag and dripped a few drops of juice onto it. "Small Doll, Small Doll, you must be thirsty. Accept my thanks."

I carefully bit off a piece of apple for her, but when I put it near her, the sandwich and juice were already gone. The doll's painted eyes had become two pinpoints of light, twinkling like stars for a moment.

"I hope this is okay," I whispered to her. "I don't have

a knife." To my relief, though, the apple disappeared as well. And then so did Small Doll.

I began looking frantically around the table and then at the floor to see if she had fallen there.

How was I going to explain to Vasilisa about losing Small Doll?

....

⤳ MISS DRAKE ⤳

I kept an eye on Nanette after she'd tried to trip Winnie. When I saw Nanette nod to Lupe, Lupe got up and went over to the table near the lunch counter and surreptitiously took one of the plastic squirt bottles of mustard before she left. A moment later, Nanette followed her.

I assumed they were up to some mischief, but since I'd seen Vasilisa's doll inside the bag, I knew she could handle the problem.

When Small Doll disappeared, poor Winnie began searching frantically. She was still looking when Mabli and Liri found her. In their hands were trays with their lunches—a hamburger for Mabli and a pizza with heaps of anchovies for Liri.

"Did you lose something?" Mabli asked.

"I . . . uh . . . lost this little wooden doll. She's this big," Winnie said, and held her thumb and forefinger apart to show how tall Small Doll was.

"Wooden?" Mabli set her tray down. "Vasilisa's your housekeeper, isn't she?"

"Yes, the doll's really hers," Winnie groaned. "I don't know what I'll do if I can't find the doll."

"Vasilisa's aunt is our housekeeper," Mabli said. "She has a Small Doll too. Don't worry. The dolls have a way of disappearing when they have an errand to run. They always pop up when they're done."

Winnie shook her head. "I'm going to keep looking anyway."

"We'll help you look as soon as we're finished. In the meantime, you might as well eat your lunch." Liri patted Winnie's lunch bag. "Hey, there's something inside."

Opening the bag, Winnie peeked inside. "It's her!"

"I told you," Mabli said as she picked up her hamburger.

After lunch, I rode upon Winnie's back as she left the cafeteria and went upstairs. Nanette and Lupe were already waiting in the hallway. Grinning as Winnie opened her

locker, they looked stunned when she began taking out her books for her afternoon classes.

Though Nanette spoke in a whisper to Lupe, I heard her with my superior hearing. "You must've gotten the wrong locker."

"I had the right one, 149," Lupe insisted.

"I'll think of something else, but next time, try to get it right." Nanette glanced at the hall clock. "We'd better get our books. We don't want to be late."

Suddenly, Nanette screamed as she backed away from her locker. Mustard dripped out of it and onto the floor. "Everything's ruined!" Hunching her shoulders, Nanette whipped around and pointed angrily at Winnie. "I don't know how, but I know you did it. I'm going straight to Ms. Griffin."

Saskia strolled over. "If you do that, I'll have to tell her that I saw Lupe take the mustard from the cafeteria."

"And you didn't warn anyone?" Mabli asked angrily.

"I knew they weren't going to try anything with me." Saskia gave a shrug. "It's up to each girl to take care of herself." She put her hand approvingly on Winnie's shoulder. "And as it turned out, Winnie could."

Nanette and Lupe were not the most popular students at Spriggs. Everyone crowded around Winnie, smiling

and patting her on the back. And Winnie, in turn, smiled back.

Yes, well done, Winnie, I thought. *You'll be all right at Spriggs after all. And well done, Small Doll. You've earned the biggest box of chocolate I can find.*

At that moment, I felt my phone vibrating. There was a new message from Reynard.

R: Traced license plate. Car rented by subsidiary that Jarvis uses 4 his dirty work.

I almost crushed the phone in my claw. I texted Reynard.

D: They must be the ones who hounded Liza and Winnie.

Warn Winnie, Reynard was quick to reply.

That would be the wisest thing to do, but seeing how happy Winnie looked, I couldn't. She was making friends and was starting to fit in at her new school.

Did I really want to spoil that? Did I want to put her on her guard and have her become the girl she had been this morning—one who retreated into an armored shell?

No.

I would fight fang and claw to let Winnie finally live the childhood she should have had—well, as normal a childhood as you can have when you live with a dragon.

Jarvis didn't realize it, but he had declared war . . . with ME!

CHAPTER FIVE

A Spriggs scholar always keeps an open mind. Try, like
Lewis Carroll's Alice, to consider six impossible things
before breakfast—or at least by lunch.

FROM THE STUDENT HANDBOOK OF THE SPRIGGS ACADEMY

∼ Winnie ∼

There are field trips, and then there are ***F*I*E*L*D T*R*I*P*S***. At the school I went to last year, we took one to a cake factory. We walked through rooms full of giant machines that stirred and squirted batter, and we'd eaten chocolate cake warm from the oven. Sweet!

But my first field trip at Spriggs sounded even better than having free cake. Lady Louhi was taking us to Loch Ness, and maybe a visit with the shyest cryptid of all: Nessie herself.

Though it was sunny and warm outside in San Francisco, we needed the jackets Lady Louhi had told us to bring. Six weeks after our first class, we'd finally gone through the portal that was the fourth classroom wall. The air in Lady Louhi's woods was cool like I think October should be, and the air smelled of the tall pine trees. Her woods could lead to anywhere, and today we were heading to the Highlands of Northern Scotland.

Lady Louhi was bringing up the rear while her animals led us along. Sassafras the Squirrel sat on the back of Emil, facing us as he held a little tour guide's yellow pennant over his head.

"This is a complete waste of time," Nanette grumbled behind me. "Just because people make up stories about some fantastic creature they say they've seen doesn't make it real. There's no scientific proof for any of these cryptids—Yeti, Bigfoot, or Nessie. I have better things to do than go on a wild-cryptid chase like this."

"Nanette should be preparing for our audition," Lupe agreed. "It's a family tradition. Her aunt Silana got into the show the first year she was eligible."

I was walking with Mabli on my left and Liri on my right. "What audition?" I whispered.

"The Halloween Festival, of course," Liri answered.

That just puzzled me even more. At my last school, for Halloween, our teacher had hung up orange paper pumpkins and the class had dressed in costumes. "There's a show?"

"And booths for games and food," Mabli explained. "It's everybody's favorite time of year. We all pitch in. We take over the auditorium, and all our families come."

"But the show is the high point of the evening," Liri added. "Only the best magical students get to display their talents."

"Well, that's one thing I don't have to worry about," I said.

"Liri and I always put our names down for the decorating committee. This year we're shorthanded," Mabli said. "We could use an artist like you."

Mabli knew I lived to draw and paint. Our art teacher had made a big fuss over my animal sketches. "Such a grasp of anatomy," she exclaimed. Well, I had been working on that since last summer when my poor misshapen drawings had come alive.

"I guess it'd be okay," I said carefully.

Suddenly Emil halted, and Sassafras began waving his pennant frantically back and forth while he held up his free paw for us to stop.

Lady Louhi called out, "Ladies, we're leaving the transition point in my forest and we're about to enter Scotland near Loch Ness. So no more bunching up like a gaggle of geese. Find a partner."

Liri tapped my shoulder. Even though she was disguised, her hand felt cool. "Partner?"

"Sure," I said as Mabli and Saskia teamed up, as did Zaina with Kari. Unlike some of the girls, I'd never been in a foreign country before. I was so excited, I didn't want to miss seeing anything.

I saw that the pine trees had begun to blur ahead of us, and about ten feet beyond that, I saw the smoky outlines of trees with flat leaves with tiny notches along the edges. A low fog crawled on all fours through the Scottish forest.

"I thought that's what might grow here," Zaina said. Her family loved to see new places and meet new people and had been to Edinburgh and Glasgow. She paused and pulled out the sheet of questions that Lady Louhi had given each of us. The first question was: *What type of tree is near the bank of the loch?*

"Alders," Zaina said as she wrote.

Since it was a group assignment, we could share answers, so I took my sheet and filled in the blank, as did others who had heard Zaina.

Liri had already answered some questions about the Loch itself. Since Liri was a naiad, she would know all about bodies of water, so I wrote down her answers:

TYPE: Freshwater
Visibility: poor because rain washes
    the peat down the valley into the
    Loch
Size/area: second-largest Loch in
    Scotland
Size/volume: Largest Loch in the British
    Isles because it is very, very, very
    deep

I remembered Lady Louhi telling us that it was claimed you could fit the population of the world ten times over in Loch Ness. She suggested we try to prove that in math class this week.

I'd just put the sheet back into my coat pocket when Lady Louhi strode to the front. "Remember, ladies, notepads and pens today," she stated firmly. "Nessie hates cameras, phones, and tablets even more than other cryptids I've met. Photographs only bring trouble and misery for a cryptid who wants her privacy intact."

Nanette's hand shot into the air and then motioned to the foggy forest. "We should go back. Nessie won't be out in this soup."

"I've been warning you that Nessie is very shy," Lady Louhi replied. "We're lucky that we're having, what the locals might call, a heavy dew. When I've brought some classes here before, it was too clear. When tour boats are loaded with Nessie seekers, she would never dare show her face."

It sounded like the tourists hunted poor Nessie like Granddad had hunted Mom and me.

"Well, maybe today's like a holiday, so she's taken the day off," Nanette suggested.

"Nanette, the journey is as worthwhile as the destination," Lady Louhi explained.

Nanette gave a sniff. "That sounds like a fortune cookie."

Lady Louhi was the most patient teacher I'd ever had. "No, it's teaching. For this field trip, you had to study, prepare, and think. You can apply those same methods to learning other things. So, even if you don't get to meet Nessie, this field trip will still be of value to you. Now do you understand?"

Nanette folded her arms. "You should've said so in the first place."

"Because it wouldn't fit on the fortune in your cookie." As the rest of us laughed, Lady Louhi reminded us, "Our assignment includes two good questions to ask Nessie. If she does appear, there'll be extra credit for the girl who asks Nessie the most interesting question."

Yesterday, we had spent the whole class going over how to behave with a cryptid and the dos and don'ts of interviewing. Proper questions to ask were ones like *Do you have any hobbies?* Improper questions were like *How much does the wart on your face weigh?*

We were each supposed to have a second question, in case someone else asked our first one before us. Like everyone else, I'd read everything in our textbook and searched the Internet but there were still humongous gaps in the information about her. I'd asked Miss Drake if she knew anything about Nessie.

As it turned out, during her travels, Miss Drake had gotten to be "chums" with Nessie, but she'd claimed that Nessie hadn't talked much about herself or her past. "A truly mysterious lady." She added, "But I remember one thing about my seaworthy friend that most people won't know."

And Miss Drake had given me a third question, just in case there was a run on my first two.

"So, my brave hearts, ready for our adventure?" Lady Louhi called, and we all nodded. She motioned us forward. "Then, onward."

The misty air collected on the alder leaves, becoming drops of water that pattered down like a light rainstorm. All of us pulled up the hoods of our coats. Only Liri didn't bother. As a naiad, water was her element, so she liked getting wet—though her cheeks plumped out as they absorbed some of the dampness.

We walked boldly into the fog. When we'd first gone through the classroom wall, I'd expected to get a headache or feel queasy, but nothing had happened. And it was the same when I stepped into Scotland. I might as well have been strolling into Golden Gate Park instead of into my first foreign country.

The path immediately began to angle down at a steep slant. I knew there were mountains behind us and on the other side of the water. We were heading into the valley, to the loch nestled between them. Beneath the dirt and leaves, I felt stepping-stones, but the moisture made them slippery. Even Emil the reindeer skidded once on a wet spot.

Ahead of me, I saw Mabli begin to slide, so I grabbed her arm to hold her up. Nanette actually did fall with a loud shout.

The noise must have startled an unseen bird, because

it fluttered its wings as it flew away, the sound moving above me and beyond. We were tucked in grayness every which way now.

"Are you all right?" Lady Louhi asked.

Lupe helped Nanette to her feet, but her skirt was as muddy as her legs. "My uniform's ruined." Nanette held her muddy arms away from her sides. "And I'm cold and wet too."

I touched my pocket, wondering if I should ask Small Doll for a favor but decided against it when Nanette snarled at me. "Wipe that grin off your face, Winnie."

"I was just going to offer you a hankie," I said, and took out a white cloth. Vasilisa had ironed it into neat squares as usual.

"Thanks," Lupe said as she took it. In just a few seconds, my handkerchief was covered in mud, but there was still a lot left on Nanette.

"You can keep the hankie," I said to Lupe.

If she threw it away, she'd be littering, so Lupe reluctantly rolled it up into a ball and tucked it into a pocket of her jacket.

After that, we eased down the trail slowly until the path finally leveled off. Not far away, we heard the sound of water lapping against the shore.

"Let's stop for a moment," said Lady Louhi, and she

called out our names one by one. When she had accounted for all of us, our teacher announced, "The fog may keep the tourists in bed this morning, but you need to see things."

She began to shake her hands slightly as if running something through a sieve while she hummed a spell. The next moment, the fog broke up into strands that streamed upward to form a dense, pearly dome with its center high above us. We could see about fifty yards—the length of a swimming pool—in front of us, and about the same distance behind us into the woods, but we couldn't see beyond that through the curving gray walls of mist. There was a pale white patch on the dome that might have been the sun trying to burn through.

I saw we were standing on a grassy area near a small cove in the long, straight loch. I couldn't see the farther shore, but I knew it was there about a mile in the distance. The loch was like a deep crack in the earth, filled in by water, formed in the valley called the Great Glen by huge glaciers during the last Ice Age.

Lady Louhi lowered her walking stick and pointed to the baskets that hung on either side of Emil's back. "You'll find tarps in the panniers so you can sit on the ground."

I got one and together with Liri, Mabli, and Saskia,

we spread the tarp out near the edge of the loch. Then, when we had sat down, we shrugged out of our backpacks.

Like everyone else, I missed the two small whiskered heads paddling toward us. They were halfway across the cove before Lady Louhi called them to our attention.

"Ah, the river folk have come to greet us," she said.

As the otters slid through the water, they bumped and patted one another as if playing tag. But they kept their heads high and their eyes facing us. They finally stopped about three yards from shore, bobbing up and down in the water as they looked us over.

I felt a tap on my shoulder. Mabli held up her work sheet and pointed at the question *What other creatures live in Loch Ness besides Nessie?* Beneath it, she'd written *Otters. Young otters are called pups or whelps.*

Mabli *would* know that detail. She liked words for their own sake and knew all sorts of old ones no one used anymore.

But I wanted to watch the otters, so I decided to fill in the answer later.

"If you see Nessie, please give her our regards, and if she's a mind for visitors, we'd love to meet her. We've brought her presents too," Lady Louhi said pleasantly to them. "In the meantime, please accept these elvers as a token of our gratitude." Yanking out a big handful of weeds, she tossed them in the air. With a few words and a wave of her stick, they changed into small eels that plopped into the water in front of the pair.

Immediately, the otters dived, popping up yards away, each with an elver in its mouth.

I could have watched them dive and eat all day, but after a few minutes, our teacher clapped her hands to get our attention. "All right, everyone. Take out the other part of your homework."

Lady Louhi had told us an old Scottish saying: *Never arrive at the door with one arm as long as the other.* What it meant was that a visitor should always bring a present. So the other half of our assignment had been to make a gift that a cryptid like Nessie might need or want.

As the otters watched us curiously, the class unsnapped backpack latches and unzipped zippers. Most had brought food appealing to a creature who lived in the water. Keona, a mermaid from Hawaii, had a quart of fresh salmon and tomato salad called *lomi-lomi*. Zaina had been very inventive with squid scones.

Lupe pulled out a large plastic globe with a half-dozen pink water lilies floating inside.

"We thought that Nessie might like a bouquet, but roses would have gotten soggy," Nanette said proudly.

"So we gathered the water lilies from my grandmother's garden pond. We thought we'd open up the globe and put these in the loch."

"Very good," Lady Louhi said, and went on to the next group. When she finally reached us, though, she stared down at the tin of sardines that Saskia had opened. My friend had stuck a toothpick in each.

Saskia tapped the label. "These are Pacific Ocean sardines, so they ought to be exotic to someone who lives in Scotland." Then she lifted one sardine by its toothpick. "And see? No muss, no fuss."

I grinned. I'd gotten used to Saskia's ways and dry humor. We got along now.

Lady Louhi looked like she was trying to keep from laughing too. "Saskia, you have a very inventive mind, but I wish you'd use it for more than inventing new ways to avoid work. Now, Mabli, where's your gift?"

Mabli tapped her forehead. "It's all up here. I found a story of a bard who stayed at Urquhart Castle here. He said Nessie came to him while he was at the shore composing a song. So I thought that maybe Nessie liked poetry."

Lady Louhi nodded approvingly. "Excellent. Something to appeal to Nessie's mind." Then she leaned forward to look at the two plastic bags that Liri and I had taken from our backpacks. "You're giving Nessie pot-pourri?"

"It's concentrated bubble bath," I explained.

Liri picked up one of the bags. "The recipe's been handed down in my family for generations. And Winnie and I spent all week finding the ingredients and then mixing soap with lavender and special calming herbs." Liri opened the bag and held it out for our teacher to smell.

I thought the scent was sweet, but Nanette pinched her nose. "The idea is to attract Nessie, not drive her away with that stink."

Surprisingly, Saskia sprang to our defense. "Nothing would smell good to you if it didn't come in a hundred-dollar bottle."

The cold, the wet, and the fall hadn't helped Nanette's mood at all. "Well, no perfume could cover up your stink, horse-girl!"

"You take that back," Saskia said.

Unfortunately, when she jumped to her feet, Saskia bumped Liri's hand and her open bag of bubble bath went flying through the air and right into the loch.

As soon as the herbs and crystals hit the water, they turned deep pink, and ribbons of pink began to wriggle quickly from the shore.

"The otters!" Lady Louhi began to raise her stick to work some spell.

"It's all right," I said. "It's supposed to be completely biodegradable and break down after an hour."

Liri nodded. "My granny promised, 'it will bother neither fish nor beast nor fowl.'"

Suddenly we heard a roar from the middle of the fog, and the mist began to swirl crazily like a steaming locomotive was coming right at us.

"But does Nessie know that?" Lady Louhi planted herself at the edge of the loch, her sturdy carved walking stick grasped in both hands, ready to defend us. "Everybody get back!"

CHAPTER SIX

~~~~~

Sharing a tasty repast can make friends
of the strangest of strangers.

～ Winnie ～

As Nessie barreled toward us, the loch itself went wild. The water in the cove rose, and a wave surged over the shore for several yards. All of us scrambled to our feet and backed up as the wave retreated, washing our tarp out into the loch along with several others.

I held my breath as a shadow grew larger and larger in the mist. The charging Nessie ripped the silvery fog into tatters. Wide, paddle-like fins drove her broad, disk-shaped body across the cove like a stone skipping over a pond. Her very long neck pointed straight at us like a spear.

As she neared the shore, Nessie rose up in the water till her head was high over ours. Her side flippers made figure eights in the water, balancing her. We could see her eyes narrow as she stared down at us. If she was trying to look fearsome, she was doing a good job. "Why did you foul the loch?" she growled in a deep voice.

As a wave of water flooded past her legs, Lady Louhi staggered but managed to stand her ground. "We're sorry. It was an accident, but we've done no harm. It's bubble bath and safe to all creatures. See?" She pointed one end of her walking stick toward the otters. Nessie's charge had churned up the bubble bath, creating patches of pink bubbles. Ready for a new game, the otters squeaked with delight as they popped the bubbles between their paws.

A lone bubble floated upward, popping against one of Nessie's nostrils. "Ha . . . ha . . . ha . . ." Nessie's head reared upward as she sneezed. "Choo."

"Gesundheit," Lady Louhi said.

Nessie arched her neck so her head was lower. Lifting a paddle fin as wide as a Prius, she dabbed the tip against her muzzle. Her fury abated, she recognized our teacher at last. "Thank ye kindly, Lady Louhi."

"I've brought another class to learn some of your great wisdom," Lady Louhi replied.

Nessie made a clicking noise as if she were chuckling. "Tish, do I look like the queen of Sheba? Ye don't have to stand up for me, gurls. Sit, sit."

The flood had swept the tarps nearest the water out onto the cove, so my friends and I had to stand but the students behind us could sit again on their dry tarps. Lucky for Liri and me, the water hadn't carried the other bath bag away. It lay on the now-muddy ground. The globe with Nanette's flowers was bobbing up and down on the cove.

Nessie noticed the tarps floating around her like broad, square leaves. "Och, but some of ye daren't, and 'tis my fault."

"It's quite all right. We'll share," Lady Louhi assured her.

By the time we sat down, Nessie had gathered up the floating tarps and laid them in a pile on the shore.

After all the excitement, I had a chance to get a real look at her. Nessie's hide was a smooth and sleek dark blue with gray spots, and her neck was long and thin like Miss Drake's, but not as elegant.

"I'm sorry, gurls, if I frightened ye," Nessie said. "Human folk began calling me Nessie, and I've come to like it even though many hear that name and imagine a scary monster. But that I'm not." She lifted her head proudly. "I'm Nessie of Loch Ness. I know every shallow cranny, every bend of the shore, every cave hidden in the murkiness below. And all the things I love and love to do make me who I am. I can hail each bird and beastie here, and they will greet me in return because they know I try to protect them."

She glanced affectionately at the otters that were splashing their paws to make more bubbles. "I've raised these wee bairns from the time they were barely weaned and I found their parents dead in a poacher's net. So now any net I find becomes torn beyond repair, and woe to the fisherman who shoots a seal because it got to a salmon afore the fisherman did. He'll soon find his boat sinking from a hole in its hull."

I wish I could tell you just how her normal voice sounded. Mabli said it was like purring, but I thought it was more like she was talking underwater, even when she wasn't. Her voice was rich, and her accent grew thick sometimes. I liked the way she rolled her *r*'s.

"Defending the loch is a worthwhile but difficult task," Lady Louhi said sympathetically.

"Made all the harder by all the folk hunting me." Nessie sighed. "Mind ye, they have nae guns, only cameras, but I don't have a moment's peace during the day."

Lady Louhi pointed to the walls of fog all around us. "For the moment, though, it's safe to relax. Won't you have some refreshment? My class made some tasty treats just for you."

Lady Louhi threw handfuls of alder leaves on the water and made them stretch wider and thinner until they were as transparent as onionskin. Yet when the class heaped the treats on them, the leaves were as sturdy as little wooden rafts. Then our teacher sent the leaf-platters streaming out in a long line until they began to circle around Nessie.

Nessie clapped her forefins together. "Lovely, lovely, but I can't stuff myself while the lassies starve."

"We brought our lunches with us," Lady Louhi said.

The flood had spoiled some lunches, but those who still had theirs shared them around.

During the flood, Emil had bounded up the path to safety. He returned now, and Sassafras climbed out of the basket where he had hidden and began to lift out bottles of spicy ginger beer and paw them out. I took one gratefully, letting the ginger beer warm and tickle my throat as I swallowed. Then I filled the bottle cap and gave Small Doll part of my sandwich.

Nessie's fins were amazing. She was able to curl just the tips to pick up a fish cake or a sardine by a toothpick.

We were too polite to count how many treats Nessie ate, but I can tell you there were lots!

When she finished, Nessie dipped her head into the loch and swung her muzzle in the water to wash it. Then, lifting her head, she nodded her thanks to us. "That was a delicious repast, lassies. My compliments to the chefs."

Nanette pointed to the globe bobbing in the cove. "We brought you flowers."

Picking up Nanette's globe with her forefins, Nessie unscrewed it and let the water lilies slide onto the water. Then, screwing up the globe again, Nessie tossed it onto the shore. "How lovely!" Nessie exclaimed as the flowers spun around like dancers for a moment.

Liri held the second bubble bath bag but was suddenly shy about calling attention to herself. So I cleared my throat then. "Liri's granny promises her bubble bath will 'ease a beastie's aches and cheer her spirits.'"

Nessie swept a fin through a pink patch of bubbles. "Doesn't that feel nice?"

Liri was still shy, so I took the bag from her and emptied it into the loch. Nessie immediately helped us along, her long tail splashing and churning the water. And with a squeak, the otters joined in until the cove was full of pink bubbles. Then, with a sigh, Nessie settled backward, ignoring Nanette's flowers. Spreading out her fins wide, she began to float. "Aye, this is just the ticket."

"Flowers and bubble bath for the weary body and poetry for the weary soul," Lady Louhi said, and motioned to Mabli. "This is Mabli. She's memorized a poem for you."

Mabli stood up and curtsied. Then, clasping her hands behind her back, she recited "To a Mouse" by Robert Burns.

"Ah, wee Bobby. Now there's a proper poet," Nessie murmured approvingly. "Well, now I've had the feeding and soothing and the listening, but ye have had none of the learning."

Lady Louhi cleared her throat. "The class does have some questions for you."

Nessie waved a forefin modestly. "You're free to waste your time as you like, but whether I'll be able to answer is another thing."

"Are you a reptile, dinosaur, or sea serpent?" Zaina asked.

Uh-oh, there went my question number one.

Nessie shook her head. "Folk like to stick a label on everything, don't they, now? What type of creature I am is not as important as who I am: a plucky lass who protects her home and those folk who kinna protect themselves."

"People would like to see you," said Kari. "If you showed yourself and told them your problems, couldn't they help you watch over the loch?"

And that was close to my question number two!

"I hope ye'll take no offense," Nessie said. "But humans are too bossy. Right now, I do what I need to do and nae anyone to second-guess me."

About a dozen other classmates asked their questions, and Nessie responded in her friendly way. Finally, Nanette spoke up. "How long have you been avoiding and tricking people?" Was she trying to get Nessie to tell us her *age*?

"Nanette!" Lady Louhi scolded sharply. "Remember what I said about improper questions?"

"I think it's a very *interesting* question," Nanette pouted. "There's nothing improper about it."

She was obviously hoping to get that extra credit, but she may have gone too far. Luckily, Nessie wasn't offended.

"I'm younger than the Loch and older than all of ye . . . even my Lady Louhi," she said coyly. "But ye must guess how I whiled away my time." Then she dipped her head in a low bow. "And now my tongue is as tired as your ears, so I'll take my leave."

I put my hand up but didn't wait for her to call on me. "Please, before you go. Would you sing us 'Molly Malone'?" *Thank you, Miss Drake!*

I watched her swivel gracefully and arch her neck down so she could study me face to face.

"Sing for my supper, hey?" Nessie asked. "And how comes it that a gurl so young knows a song so old?"

"A friend told me you like it" was all I said.

"*Your* friend, is she?" Nessie asked thoughtfully. "Then I've no choice but to sing the little ditty about the Irish gurl. It's written by a fellow Scot, or so they say." Tilting back her head, she began to sing:

> *"In Dublin's fair city,*
> *Where the girls are so pretty,*
> *I first set my eyes on sweet Molly Malone*
> *As she wheeled her wheelbarrow,*
> *Through streets broad and narrow,*
> *Crying, 'Cockles and mussels, alive, alive O!*
> *Alive, alive O!*

Alive, alive O!'
Crying, 'Cockles and mussels, alive, alive O!' "

If you'd heard her, I think you'd be surprised. Her voice was truly sweet and much higher than her speaking voice. It rippled or trilled so that some words had many, many notes. I don't think any human could sing that way.

She paused between verses to tell us, as if we were young otters who needed teaching, "Cockles are saltwater clams. I have never tasted them, but the gulls who visit the loch say they are very tasty."

Then she lifted her head again and sang in her soft, gentle voice that would have been drowned out by the breeze to anyone farther away.

"She was a fishmonger,
But sure 'twas no wonder,
For so were her father and mother before,
And they both wheeled their barrows,
Through the streets broad and narrow,
Crying, 'Cockles and mussels, alive, alive O!' "

"Come sing the chorus with me," she said, tossing her head. And we did . . . as well as we could.

"'Alive, alive O!
Alive, alive O!'
Crying, 'Cockles and mussels, alive, alive O!'"

"Ah, *gur-r-rls*," she said, trilling her *r*'s, her accent growing stronger with emotion. "My pipes are a wee bit rusty, but that was a bonnie thing to do. And best if I stop here. The next verse makes me blub like a babe in arms, and I'll not have any sadness on such a pleasant day."

"I've learned something new and interesting about you," Lady Louhi said with satisfaction. "So extra credit for Winnie."

"Interesting gurls ask the most interesting questions, don't they, though?" Nessie observed.

From the corner of my eye, I saw Nanette practically grinding her teeth. But then Nessie began studying me, and I felt like I was under a microscope. Finally, she gestured a forefin at me. "Come closer, Winnie gurl."

I looked at her, large and grand. She was no longer the strange creature in the fuzzy online photos. She was no more a monster to me now than my own dragon was. They just were who they were. So I took a step.

"Closer," Nessie said.

I shuffled forward until the water's edge was only inches from my shoes.

"For the sake of our common friend, I'll do a fore-telling for ye," Nessie said. Her head hovered close to mine. Her pupils seemed as large as platters—and black, blacker than ink, blacker than shadow, blacker than even the bottom of the loch where the sun never reaches. My reflection floated alone in that darkness, every detail sharp and clear.

Her voice became deeper than before, and it seemed to bounce inside me like I was as hollow as a drum, feeling as if each word was being carved inside me as she spoke them. "I ken ye are a plucky lass just like me and share my fate. We kinna twiddle our fins when our homes and loved ones are in danger. Ye shall also be the shield against the arrow, the locked door against the wolf, the stout wall against the flood."

Then, bending her head slightly, she carefully brushed her head against my cheek. The touch of her slick, damp skin felt almost like a kiss.

When she raised her head, it felt like a spell had been broken. I blinked, feeling like I had just woken up from a dream. I sort of remember Lady Louhi bowing to Nessie and saying, "Thank you, Nessie. You are a Scottish treasure, and it's been an honor for all of us to meet you. You've given my students much to ponder and made their outing one they will remember . . . as you always do."

"And now I must take my leave," Nessie said. "Thank ye, gurls, for the lovely gifts of the food, the sweet scents, and even sweeter words. They were all soothing to an old gurl like meself."

Then, with easy strokes of her fins, she circled around and drifted out of the cove and back into the mist, and the otters went with her.

The sun was beginning to set as we followed Emil and Sassafras up the path. In the twilight, the yellow triangle of Sassafras's pennant was easy to follow.

As we climbed, I wondered what I could do if trouble came. I was just a kid, not a powerful creature like Nessie or a dragon like Miss Drake.

"What do you think Nessie meant?" I asked my friends.

Saskia shrugged. "It was her way of saying you were brave, that's all."

But I couldn't get Nessie's words out of my head. So I dropped back along the line to the rear where Lady Louhi was and asked her about Nessie's prophecy.

"She was looking far ahead into your future," Lady Louhi assured me. "Perhaps you'll be a police officer or a soldier or lawyer."

As we walked through the fourth wall and into the classroom, we heard the class bell ringing to go on to the next period. I glanced at the clock. The whole outing had taken minutes, not hours, in school time.

Lady Louhi called loudly from behind us, "Your work sheets are due tomorrow. Don't forget to read chapters fifteen and sixteen."

I was still worrying about Nessie's prediction as I followed my friends out of class. When the bell rang for the next period, I realized everyone was gone. I was in such a hurry to catch up to them that I went around a corner too fast and bumped into Sir Isaac.

In one hand, he held a plastic cage with a toad inside it, and in the other, he had a pomegranate. I couldn't begin to figure out how he was going to use them in our science class, but it probably was going to be spectacular.

"Ah, Burton, was your jaunt to Loch Ness fruitful?" he asked.

I felt like this might be another of Sir Isaac's trick questions. He was a master at it.

"There weren't any pomegranates if that's what you mean, Sir Isaac," I said.

The corners of Sir Isaac's mouth curled up ever so slightly. I'd learned by now that was equal to a big grin from most other people. "As literal as ever, Burton. That's just the right answer for a budding scientist."

"I'm not a budding scientist," I told him as firmly as I could.

"Not yet." There was a twinkle in his eyes. "But give me time, and you will be."

That's what he thinks! "Do you believe in prophecies, Sir Isaac?" I asked, and told him about Nessie's foretelling and what Lady Louhi thought it meant.

I expected him to tell me that I could ignore it, but instead he nodded. "Nessie knows the company you keep: Miss Drake suffers neither fools nor cowards lightly. And so Nessie extrapolated from those known facts and came up with a hypothesis. So perhaps you will be a forensic scientist helping the police."

I had a nagging feeling that Nessie had been talking about a time closer than before I grew up. Maybe Miss Drake would know what her old friend meant.

CHAPTER SEVEN

A wise pet may do as she is told . . .
but usually in her own fashion.

∽ MISS DRAKE ∽

After I had escorted Winnie home from school, I circled around through my secret entrance to my apartment and resumed my regular size. I must say that all this stretching and shrinking was making me feel a bit elastic.

As usual, I'd already laid out tea, but this was a special one in honor of Winnie's field trip. The

four-layer server was filled with scones and small sand-wiches on the coffee table along with a big bowl of clot-ted cream and a big pot of lingonberry jam.

Normally Winnie tucked right in to her tea as she told me all about her classes and what her friends had said and done. Having friends was still as strange and fun to her as the things she did in her school courses. Today, I thought she would chatter on endlessly.

But Winnie was oddly silent as she stared at the tray.

I suspected that Nanette had been up to mischief. "Was there any trouble with your classmates?" I hinted.

She shrugged. "No, of course not."

From the very first day, Winnie had insisted that everything at Spriggs had gone smoothly—even though I myself had witnessed the tiffs with Nanette. I sus-pected Winnie was trying hard to keep her promise to her mother to stay out of fights. I had tried to respect Winnie's silence, but perhaps I'd let it go on too long.

However, before I could press her, Winnie asked, "You know Nessie pretty well, don't you? Can she pre-dict the future?"

I straightened in surprise. "What happened?"

When Winnie told me about a foretelling for a "plucky lass," I realized I may have made a bad mistake suggest-ing Winnie ask Nessie to sing her favorite song.

The last thing I'd expected was for the singing to lead

to a foretelling. Nessie only used the Sight for her closest friends, not a natural she had just met. "It's my fault she talked about arrows and wolves and floods. I forgot how morbid the last verse makes her."

Had Nessie really felt some kinship with Winnie? Or had she done it as a favor to me? Whatever the truth, I was sure that Lady Louhi and Sir Isaac had the right of it: protecting people lay many years ahead of Winnie.

"She didn't finish the song, because she said it was too sad," Winnie said.

"The ending *is* sad, but it's all part of the story and very lovely in its own right," I said. I got up and chose a large flat disc from the rows of discs in my cabinet. I delicately placed it inside my music box and turned the handle round and round to wind it up.

Despite her worries, Winnie smiled, watching the disc spin gracefully. "I love how the music sounds like tinkling bells." I'd always thought of it as music played by an elfin orchestra that gifted artisans had delightfully captured in their mechanical wonder.

I'd never sung for Winnie before. My voice wasn't nearly as sweet as Nessie's, so I tried to sing with great feeling. I felt a tear start to form in the corner of my eye, and I caught the pearl in my paw in mid-verse.

"She died of a fever,
And no one could save her,
And that was the end of sweet Molly Malone.
But her ghost wheels her barrow,
Through streets broad and narrow,
Crying, 'Cockles and mussels, alive, alive O!'"

As the music box played, Winnie joined me in the chorus.

"'Alive, alive O!
Alive, alive O!'
Crying, 'Cockles and mussels, alive, alive O!'"

"You see? That final part puts everyone into a somber mood." I set the pearl on the coffee table. It was the same blue as Nessie. "It makes me cry dark pearls and makes Nessie paint her predictions in dark hues."

With a claw, I sliced a scone open then and put it on a small plate that I handed to Winnie. "Nessie was only speaking in metaphors, so don't be a silly goose. Put those arrows, wolves, and floods right out of your mind and enjoy your tea instead."

"Lighten up, you mean," Winnie said, already feeling better.

"Exactly," I said as she began to spread jam over the scone.

....

∽ Winnie ∽

The next day, Ms. Kululu passed out fancy note cards to each of us in English class. On the front was a drawing of our beloved mascot on the gate, a gargoyle we all called Mortimer, and the words THE SPRIGGS ACADEMY. The gold words were raised and puffy.

"Today we will be writing notes to Nessie," she told us. "You can say thank you in person or on the phone, but I believe the nicest way is to send a handwritten note.

"Mention something Nessie did that was special to you, and thank her for it," she continued. "Take your time and write carefully. A thank-you note is your gift to repay a kindness given to you, and neat penmanship makes for a nicer gift."

"Excuse me, Ms. Kululu, but may I use *my own* stationery?" Nanette sounded like she didn't expect our teacher to refuse. "I have my cards made by the same printer who does the school cards." She gave a slight toss of her head. "They're the best in San Francisco after all."

Opening her bag, Nanette took out a card and held it up. The light shone off her golden family crest and her name in extremely fancy letters. It made me want to run my fingers over the surface, but I'd never give her the satisfaction of asking if I could.

Anyway, it's not the card that's important. It's what you write in it.

Everyone started the assignment but me. I wanted to ask Nessie if she had seen something bad ahead for me, but that didn't seem like much of a thank-you. And I had another problem.

I don't mind writing at home, but I hate having to write in class, when I'm under pressure. Then I realized I could do something else and make that my gift. I opened the card and drew a picture of Nessie, the otters, and myself on the bottom half. Under my drawing, I wrote:

Dear Nessie,
Your singing was lovely. I'll always remember my day with you. Thank you.
                    Your friend, Winnie

"That's charming, and so very *you*, Winnie," said Ms. Kululu as she passed by, checking to see how and what we were doing. "When you finish, girls, seal the envelopes and give your notes to Lady Louhi. She'll make sure Nessie gets them."

When she had moved on, I quickly drew another figure on the top half of the card—Miss Drake with a cup of tea in her paw.

I popped my card into the envelope and sealed it before anyone else could see. But I smiled to myself, thinking my drawing of Miss Drake would make a nice surprise for Nessie.

....

∽ MISS DRAKE ∽

It was a lot easier to deal with villains in the old days. A couple of quick chomps and the world was suddenly a better place. And, depending on what country I was in, a tiger, lion, bear, or wolf would get the credit.

But nowadays there are pesky coroners with microscopes who raise all sorts of awkward questions. Humans like to think they're always improving things, but in this case, all they did was make it harder to get rid of evildoers.

From Rivera, I knew Jarvis's thugs had taken a room

in a motel on Lombard Street near the Golden Gate Bridge. Tourists favored the motels, so the pair would pass unnoticed.

So far, the thugs had simply observed Winnie and her mother, Liza. I think Jarvis had expected Liza would waste all her newfound money on extravagant luxuries so he would have the ammunition he needed to take Winnie away.

He'd misjudged Liza so badly—it was as if he didn't know his daughter at all. Instead of hearing that Liza was wasteful and negligent, he had gotten reports of a woman who worked hard at her job and who then came home to be a devoted mother. Any father but Jarvis would have been proud of her.

Of course, Jarvis's spies had no idea *they* were being spied on. My friends took shifts observing so there were eyes constantly on them. Perhaps a pigeon flapping over their SUV. Or a seagull on a telephone wire watching them grab a bite at a fast food restaurant. Or an intrepid spider dangling in a corner of their room whose many eyes saw all the passwords they used on their laptop.

I had figured that it was only a matter of time before Jarvis finally lost his patience and ordered his thugs to do something more drastic. Three days after Winnie had visited Nessie, Rivera had finally sent word to Reynard that the thugs had left the motel dressed all in black and had stolen a van belonging to the gas and electric company.

Reynard suspected they would try to invade the house soon to plant bugs and cameras so they could spy on Liza and Winnie.

Jarvis had always been determined to get what he wanted no matter the cost. When he was small, he'd been a horrible little despot to his entire family. And he hadn't stopped there. Sly, mean, greedy, he'd terrorized the other children in the neighborhood.

The only one able to get Jarvis to stop was Fluffy. All she had to do was whisper one word in his ear, and he would stop misbehaving. Somehow Fluffy had found out a secret that Jarvis did not want others to know.

Of course, I'd asked Fluffy what the word was. But Fluffy insisted that she'd promised Jarvis not to tell anyone else, and as sweet as Fluffy was, she could also be very stubborn. I could never pry the secret word out of her. Nor was I ever to eavesdrop when Fluffy was whispering the word to Jarvis. I tried listening spells, but I could never quite make out what she was saying.

In my frustration, I imagined the secret was all sorts of crimes—a stolen jewel, maybe even someone's murdered pet, dead and buried in the garden, because I wouldn't put anything past Jarvis. And then Fluffy had taken the knowledge with her when she passed away.

If only she had realized how much Winnie would need that word now. Life would be so much simpler if we could make Jarvis behave.

Vasilisa's polite knock broke my reveries. "Miss Drake, there is a message from Nessie," she said, her voice muffled by the wood.

"Slip it under the door," I ordered.

"She sent a messenger who has to tell it to you personally," Vasilisa explained.

When I had opened the door, I saw Vasilisa with a tired-looking thrush perched on her wrist. As soon as he saw me, the thrush fluttered his wings and straightened up. "My mistress sends her thanks to the interesting one called Winnie. She loves the drawings."

Nessie must have had some magic of her own to be able to send the thrush here so quickly. "I'll give Winnie the message."

"She also sent a foretelling for you, Miss Drake," the thrush said. It shifted its claws on Vasilisa's wrist and recited: "When the strong are the weakest and the weakest the strongest, the lost will be found and the found will be lost."

Remember Delphi and do not lose your temper, I

reminded myself. Two thousand five hundred years ago, I had scolded the Oracle for not getting straight to the point, but some prophets cannot take constructive criticism. I nearly lost my hide getting out of there and didn't dare set a paw in Greece for a hundred years after that.

So I thanked the thrush politely and then nodded to Vasilisa. "Will you see that our guest has food and rest?"

"I wouldn't mind a worm or two," the thrush ventured.

"Of course," Vasilisa said calmly as if she served live worms every day.

Later that evening, I had plenty of time to ponder Nessie's foretelling as I waited for Jarvis's thugs. When Nessie talked about the weakest, did she mean Small Doll? But what could Small Doll do? Tickle Jarvis with a feather duster?

Speculation was a useless exercise. I would trust to my own wits and power to deal with problems—just like now.

Shrunk to a foot in length and unseen from the street, I crouched on the roofline. Near me, the banner with the family's crest of three dragons flapped like a battle flag, but I was sorry the government had done away with fog-horns. Their bellows reminded me of the dragon watch calling out the time and that all was well. When I was a hatchling, I couldn't get to sleep until I heard them begin their rounds.

Beneath me, Winnie, Vasilisa, and Liza slept, and Vasilisa's doll dusted and swept, trusting me to keep them safe. I would not fail them.

We had installed a sophisticated electronic security system on the entry points into the house, but I was sure that Jarvis's thugs were skilled enough to get around the house's human-designed defenses.

If I were going to break into a heavily defended home, this would be the kind of night I'd pick. A thick, low fog had rolled in, making it hard to see anything on the ground or the stars and moon above. Yet living as drag-ons often do, deep in the sea where the sun never shines, my eyes can easily see in what would be darkness to a human.

The cars parked in the street looked like the sil-houettes of slumbering sheep, and the garden's bushes looked like cutouts that appeared and disappeared in the drifting mist.

Nor in fog like this could I expect any help from the creatures and spirits of the hilltop. Birds huddled in their nests, flower spirits drowsed, leaves curled around them.

But in the backyard I saw the top of the young redwood tree where Paradise napped, hidden but ready to wake and come to defend our home if I summoned her.

The invaders moved stealthily for humans, but I detected the faint clink of metal, the sound of the cloth of their sneakers crushing the damp grass, their panting breath. I couldn't see them, though, until the thugs were halfway to the house. By the time I woke Paradise, they could be breaking into my home. What if Winnie heard them and came to investigate?

So I decided to handle them myself. The very same fog that hid them would hide me in my small form. I launched myself from the roof, gliding downward through the mist.

As I drew close, I saw the silhouette of a muscular man crawling. He was wearing a black turtleneck and slacks, and a belt with many bulging pouches that likely held his spy instruments.

"Hey, Pete, there's a bat over your head," whispered the second invader.

Too late, I saw the devices strapped to their faces. Two red circles burned hot and fierce as tiny coals. With a shock, I realized just how badly I'd underestimated

Jarvis. He'd outfitted his team with thermal imaging scopes that would let them see in the dark just as well as I did.

Rolling over on his back, Pete pulled a steel cylinder about a foot long from his belt and gave a flick of his wrist. Instinct made me bank sharply to the left. *Sproing!* It was one of those expandable metal batons.

Instantly, the cylinder shot out to two feet in length. It swished through the air as he swung it at me, but I was already darting behind a shrub.

"I hate bats, Abe," the first thug said.

"Yeah?" Abe asked. "I think the feeling is mutual. Come on. We got a whole house to bug."

I should have been glad they had mistaken me for a bat, and yet I found it insulting. But this was no time for a zoology lesson. I shrank to the size of a bee and darted back over the lawn. They had almost reached the house by then.

The flakes of dandruff in Pete's hair looked as big as serving platters as I hovered over his head. I gathered up the gas in one of my stomachs and then dived past his forehead and onto his goggles.

When I was a hatchling, I'd taken "firsts" in my fire lessons, and I've been adding to and perfecting my technique ever since. It all comes down to controlling the gas in my stomach and breath control. Or, as Sir Walter Scott inelegantly put it after I had demonstrated for him, dragons were like leathery bagpipes.

Pursing my lips now, I blew out fire at the lowest temperature I dared so the flame itself would be a broad one. Then I twisted my head so the flame would sweep in front of both goggles.

"Argh!" Pete cried out. "My eyes!"

The big baby. I hadn't touched his eyes, just momentarily blinded him.

When he reached his hand up, it looked as big as a hill. He snatched the goggles up over his head, but I was already zipping toward Abe. He was shorter than Pete but even more muscular.

"What happened?" Abe asked as I perched on his goggles.

Next, he was rolling around and yanking off his goggles too.

I returned to Pete, who had somehow kept hold of his baton. Try to strike me, will he? A burst of flame heated the steel, and he howled, instantly dropping the baton.

With them temporarily unable to see me, and Pete disarmed, it was time to get to my real work. Among dragons, I'm noted for my skill in reducing the length of my flame to a few millimeters. The microbursts burned as hot as an acetylene torch and easily cut through their gear belts without even singeing the cloth beneath.

Even if the invaders could have seen me, they wouldn't have appreciated the artistry and variety of my fire. Lancelike tongues of flame applied to their posteriors got them to their feet. Needle-thin flames nipped at their ankles as I drove them like a sheepdog herding two very stupid sheep. They stumbled blindly across the lawn, down the driveway, and along the sidewalk until they bumped into their SUV. Panting, they slumped to the pavement.

"What was that?" Pete asked, blinking his eyes.

"Maybe some sort of defensive microlasers," Abe said, rubbing his own eyes.

"Whatever it is, Mr. Granger can't pay me enough to go near that place again," Pete said.

"Ditto," Abe said.

I settled on the fence, watching as they regained their eyesight, and waited to see if they changed their minds. But they couldn't wait to tumble into their SUV and escape.

I grew to falcon size, fetched the goggles and gear belts, and hid them. Then I returned to the roof to keep guard. I kept my vigil the rest of the night, but there was no more trouble. Not surprisingly, I was yawning early the next morning in the kitchen as I told Paradise, Vasilisa, and her doll about my encounter.

I was only about a foot high as I sat upon the table, so my cup of tea was as big as a cauldron. "By the way, you'll find some night goggles under a shrub," I told Paradise. "Maybe they'll help you catch that gopher you've been complaining about."

Despite the gifts, Paradise folded her arms disapprovingly. "You should have called me, Miss Drake."

Forepaws on the rim of the cup and standing on my hind paws, I lowered my head and sipped some of the hot tea to calm my stomachs. Breathing fire always unsettles them a bit. "They'd gotten too close to the house, and I was able to handle them myself."

Vasilisa frowned as if her soufflé had just fallen. "It would have taken them a while to disable the security. Paradise could have distracted them while you attacked. You made a big mistake by not calling us."

I straightened so fast that I tipped the cup, spilling tea onto the table. "No one asked for your opinion."

"So?" Vasilisa folded her arms. "I will give it anyway. Do not make a bigger mistake. Tell the Little Madame about her grandfather."

"You haven't heard Winnie talk about the days when she and her mother were on the run," I argued. "It would only make her worry again. So we're going to have to be especially watchful from now—" I broke off as I heard Winnie's footsteps in the hallway.

A moment later, Winnie came through the door.

Though she'd only been at Spriggs a few months, my dear pet looked happier and much more relaxed. She was even wearing her beret at a jaunty angle. I couldn't let her grandfather take that *joie de vivre* away from her.

Winnie saw the extra cup and me next to it. "Oh, good. You're all here. Vasilisa and Paradise, you should come to the Halloween Festival with Miss Drake." She bowed to Vasilisa's doll. "And you too, Small Doll."

"I'm afraid I'll be busy, Miss Winnie," Paradise said. If it wasn't foggy, she, Vasilisa, and Small Doll would have more than enough to deal with at home.

"But you're part of our family now," Winnie argued.

Vasilisa cleared her throat. "On Halloween, we get our share of pranksters, Little Madame. We'll need to stay here."

Winnie turned to me. "Tell them to come."

I looked pointedly. "I leave the house to Vasilisa and the grounds to Paradise, and they leave the bigger decisions to me."

Winnie thought for a moment. "Well, there's supposed to be lots of snacks and treats at the Festival. I'll be sure to bring back a goody bag for each of you." When she saw the gleam in the doll's eyes, she added, "And an extra special bag for you."

"By the way," I said, trying to sound as casual as I could, "Nessie liked the drawing you sent."

"Cool." Picking up the doll carefully, she slipped her into a pocket and then glanced at the clock. "Oh no, look at the time!" Snatching her lunch bag, she ran from the kitchen.

As I got ready to follow, Paradise predicted, "Things are getting serious. You're going to have to warn her eventually."

"Yes, Miss Drake. Do not underestimate the Little Madame." Vasilisa's palm slapped the table for emphasis. "She may worry, but she is a warrior."

I had a bad feeling they were right. Yet as I rose from the table, I insisted, "I know she's strong and tough, because she's had to fight all her life up until now. But she shouldn't have to do that anymore. The worst thing she should worry about is being late for school, not escaping from a pack of bloodhounds. I want her to stay a child as long as we can manage it."

CHAPTER EIGHT

*Remember, even the brightest pet makes
a mess of things every now and then.*

∼ MISS DRAKE ∼

That afternoon after school, I thought, *No matter
how many keys to my door I con-
fiscated from Winnie, she always
seemed to have another.*

"Just how many keys do you
have?" I asked as I heard her
open the no longer locked
door.

"If you guess right, I'll
turn them all in." She liked
playing games with me.

"Seventeen," I hazarded.

She made a buzzing noise. "*Ennh*. Wrong."

"Twenty," I said.

Winnie shook her head. "You only get one try a day."

In her arms was a box of paper, paints, and brushes. Where other children would have filled their rooms with toys and clothes, Winnie spent her allowance on art supplies.

"What's that for?" I asked.

"I volunteered for the decorating committee for the Halloween Festival." She dropped the box on top of my priceless Bokhara. "I need to get started right away."

I had been so occupied with Jarvis and his thugs that I had forgotten about Halloween. At Spriggs, it was as big a holiday as Christmas.

With a hind paw, I gently shoved the box off my carpet and onto the floorboards. "Why can't you do that in your room?"

Winnie spread out two sheets of black paper on the coffee table alongside some brushes. "Because you'll get into the holiday spirit, too, if you make decorations with me."

"Nonsense," I snapped. "I have enough spirit for a coven of witches."

Picking up a paintbrush, she tapped the sheet in front of me. "I need a pumpkin on this one. The clubs are in charge of the big, fancy displays. My committee fills in the small stuff."

A few minutes later, I stared down at the drops of orange paint that Winnie had spattered on my Bokhara. "I'll never be able to get those stains out," I grumbled.

"The paint will come right off." Wetting a finger, she rubbed the spot vigorously. When she lifted her finger, though, the dot had turned into a stripe. "Oops. I'll get a damp towel."

I held up my paws, worried that she would turn the stripe into an orange circle the size of Hawaii. "No, no, I'm sure Vasilisa's doll can clean it if I ask her for help."

An hour later, Winnie stared critically at a dozen pictures of pumpkins drying around my living room. "Hmm, maybe if I put the ones you did in dark corners, people won't mistake them for suns."

I picked up the damp brushes, holding my free paw underneath them to catch the drips. "I never said I was an artist. Pumpkins are for pie, not for decorating."

Winnie whirled around. "But you'll come to the Festival anyway, right?"

I saw her bright eyes and big grin. Fluffy used to get just as excited. "I wouldn't miss it," I promised.

"Please, please, please, can Mom come too?" Winnie begged. "I know she'll love it."

Most of the natural parents who send their children

to Spriggs already know about magicals, because they do business with the clans. But there are a few exceptions who are kept ignorant for various reasons—like a reporter for a national news network who didn't realize he had married an elf. Using their connections, her clan had his network send him to do a feature story in Malaysia or Timbuktu, and he would miss the Festival each time.

"Ah," I said.

"Does that still mean we can't tell her?" Winnie asked, disappointed.

I took the brushes into the kitchen and cleaned them in the sink and then put the kettle on to boil. I had been observing Liza carefully these last couple of months. She seemed like a calm, levelheaded woman who didn't panic easily when her life took sudden twists and turns. Now seemed like the time to let her know part of the truth.

I wiped my hands on a towel as I came back into the room. "We'll need to prepare your mother first for some of the magic she'll see. She's too smart to think it'll all be special effects and holograms and lasers."

Winnie breathed a sigh of relief. "I was going to explode if I had to keep quiet a day longer."

"Well, if you feel yourself about to burst, please step away from the carpet." I draped the towel over my shoulder. "I think we should still keep *me* a secret. I meant, we could let your mother know a bit about magicals so she won't be surprised when she meets the other parents at the Festival."

Winnie grinned. "You mean when one of them turns into a bat?"

"Bats are the least of our worries," I said, thinking of past Festivals I had attended with Fluffy and Caleb, her father. Jarvis had always been left home with his mother, neither of whom had wanted to go to Spriggs functions—Jarvis because it was an all-girls school and Mary because it was too progressive for its time. She would have had a hysterical fit if she'd known about the magicals. "When they clap, zombies are always losing a few spare parts, and everyone has to help find them and then glue them back together."

"I don't think Mom would freak out," Winnie insisted.

"She's certainly tough," I said, "and she's also smart enough to know that there's more to the world than what we usually see."

"But . . ." Winnie hesitated.

I could guess her doubts. "But what happens if she doesn't handle the truth well? You would have to transfer to a regular human school."

Winnie suddenly looked upset. "I don't want to leave Spriggs."

I put a foreleg around her and gave her a gentle squeeze. "She's met your friends, hasn't she?"

"Sure," Winnie said. "They've been here for sleepovers."

"So I have an idea how we can make the truth easier to digest," I said. "Here's what you do. . . ."

ᗡᡣᡣᡉ Winnie ᗡᡣᡣᡉ

"You're coming to the Halloween Festival, right?" I asked Mom. We were in the kitchen that Saturday morning getting lunch ready for my friends. Vasilisa would have done it, but Mom had insisted on giving her the day off. Even then, Mom had to shove Vasilisa out the door.

Mom began cutting up tomatoes. "Of course, but what do you want to be?"

"The ghost of Molly Malone," I said.

"Who?" Mom asked.

"She's from an old song," I explained as I spread mustard on the bread. "I've already sketched out my costume.

Just a simple blouse and long skirt with patches. She sold cockles and mussels, so I'll wear a shell necklace."

"I can help you with that." Mom was warming to the idea. "And I saw a ghost makeup kit in the drugstore."

"What would you like to be?" I asked. I started to put the slices of Appenzeller cheese and tomatoes on the bottom bread slice.

"A witch, of course," Mom said, "with some green makeup, maybe a wart or two." She was growing excited. "I'll make the dress, and I'll get a pointy hat to go with it."

Oh boy. Real witches had stopped wearing pointy hats three centuries ago. And some of the witches at school were even worse fashion snobs than Nanette. It was going to be a job keeping Mom from insulting them or their families.

At lunchtime, I brought the sandwiches while Mom carried the tray with the pitcher of iced tea and empty plates and glasses.

Liri, Mabli, Zaina, and Saskia were sitting in the living room watching the sailing boats in the bay. At this distance, they looked like toys on sparkling glass. Sheets of poster board were stacked up in the corner, and there were plastic bins with paints, markers, and everything else we'd need. When we started working, we'd shift everything up to my bedroom. Small Doll had cleaned it so many times this week that I doubted if there was a speck of dust or piece of lint there.

As Mom set the tray down on the coffee table, she admired the view. "We've never spent a fall anywhere that was like San Francisco."

Though we were three weeks into October, the sky was sunny, and the temperature was in the high sixties.

"You can't beat it," Saskia said.

"Well, I'll leave you girls to make your plans," Mom said.

"Wait, Mom." I glanced at the others to see if they were ready. They all nodded. So I got to the real point of the get-together. "Mom, you know how much I love Spriggs, but it's a little different from the other schools I've gone to."

Mom laughed. "Not many schools would offer the history of magic, but Ms. Griffin explained it was an interdisciplinary way to learn about science, language, and history with a little PE thrown in."

"Well, the students are a little special too," I said.

Mom shrugged. "It's what's inside that counts. You know that."

"I'm glad you feel that way." Twisting around, I motioned to my classmates. "My friends are all magicals. Mabli's a dwarf and Saskia is part centaur, so that's why she's so good with horses." Then I nodded at Liri. "And Liri's a water sprite."

The next moment, Liri had become a transparent, silvery form. The sun came through the picture window and hit her perfectly, raising a rainbow in the mist around her.

"And Zaina's a djinn," I said.

Zaina rose in a tan cloud that sort of held her usual shape, but the sand kept swirling around restlessly inside the network of fiery veins that formed her face.

Mom's mouth opened and closed several times as if she kept changing her mind about what to say.

"I know it's a lot to take in," I said gently. "Just remember what Great-Aunt Amelia used to write us—that the world was a lot more wonderful than most people realized. I think she was trying to prepare us for something like this."

Mom stared at me, a little angry now as well as puzzled. "How long have you known?"

Miss Drake had coached me how to answer this question. It was close to the truth. Miss Drake had thought that for Mom's sake—as well as her own—close enough was good enough for now. "Since I started at Spriggs.

Magicals keep their identities hidden so we humans don't pick on them. It's important we keep quiet about this, Mom. There's a lot at stake."

Pearl-like bubbles rose in Liri's throat. "Please."

Zaina drifted around. "Yes, please."

Saskia and Mabli both added their *please*s as well.

"Well, I can understand being picked on because you're different," Mom grunted, and then eyed me. "But I don't like the fact that you kept it secret from me."

"I'm sorry, Mom," I said, "but I was trying to be careful."

Mom looked at Mabli. "Is your aunt Dylis a dwarf too?"

"Yes," Mabli answered.

"And she's helped us a lot," I reminded Mom. "So you won't tell anyone?"

"They're your friends." Mom shook her head. "I wouldn't risk hurting them."

I breathed a sigh of relief. "Thanks, Mom."

....

ᨒ MISS DRAKE ᨒ

Late that evening as Winnie slipped into my rooms, I set out the plate of flower-shaped cookies.

"There's mint chocolate chip ice cream in the freezer. I thought we could either celebrate or commiserate tonight. Which is it?"

Winnie picked up a cookie and tossed it into her mouth. Through a mouthful of crumbs, she announced, "It's party time. Mom took it very well."

"And did she promise not to tell anyone about the magicals?" I asked.

Winnie nodded. "Yep."

I sighed inwardly with relief. Not all naturals can accept the fact that magicals live among them. Old superstitions about us die hard. "You should have had more faith in your mother, Winnie."

Winnie's hand hovered over the plate of cookies. "Me? You're the one who wouldn't let me tell her about magicals before," she protested.

I rose to get the ice cream. "Now, now, it's only the small-minded who rewrite history."

Winnie grabbed a handful of cookies this time. "Well, when are we going to tell her about you, huh?"

"In the fullness of time, of course," I said, and stepped into the kitchen.

CHAPTER NINE

~⌇⌇⌇~

By cultivating a creative spirit in work and play,
a Spriggs-ian will never be dull or dreary.

FROM THE STUDENT HANDBOOK OF THE SPRIGGS ACADEMY

~⌇ Winnie ⌇~

The week before Halloween, things got kind of crazy at Spriggs. As long as the joke wasn't cruel and no one was physically hurt, there was a tradition of students playing pranks on their teachers. When our English teacher, Ms. Kululu, tried to read a sonnet out loud, she discovered that some joker had substituted *Best Knock-Knock Jokes of 1985* for her textbook.

And our social studies teacher, Mr. Ramirez, discovered his model of a California mission had been rented out to a family of field mice. The fake landlady turned out to be Saskia, so Ms. Griffin let the mice take over part of Saskia's locker for the rest of the year.

Sir Isaac was the most popular target, because he was also the hardest to trick. He seemed to have a sixth sense about practical jokes. Buckets of water wet the floor rather than him; his laser pointer, painted by a jokester with an invisible chemical that should have blackened his hand, blackened a rubber glove instead. He even egged the pranksters on by reviewing the practical jokes like he was a movie critic.

On Wednesday, he held up the small striped snake by its tail. "Fie on thee! Fie! A garter snake in my desk drawer? I'm appalled by your lack of imagination, which I blame on too much television, computer games, and sugary treats." He let the snake curl around his wrist. "However, a good teacher can turn anything into a learning experience."

And he proceeded to give a short lecture on *Thamnophis sirtalis tetrataenia* as he walked from table to table making sure we each looked eyeball to beady little eyeball with the snake. It didn't bother me, but several girls squirmed in their seats and one looked ready to run out of the classroom.

When the last class bell rang, Spriggs filled with the sound of hammers and saws as the clubs began to assemble the stalls for food and games. All week long, the smell of poster paint drifted through the hallways.

The magical acts got to practice on the stage in the auditorium. The high school and middle school performers would come later in the evening, and by tradition the most promising elementary witch or sorceress would begin the show. So it was a big deal when Nanette was chosen.

As for my friends and me, we had our hands full decorating the school, especially when the magic jack-o'-lantern wouldn't cooperate. It was an orange porcelain sphere about three feet in diameter and a gift from the class of '39. By another Spriggs tradition—boy, we had a lot of them—it always sat on a table to the left of the auditorium doors. The jack-o'-lantern was supposed to yell "Boo!" but instead kept singing "Danny Boy."

Finally, I lifted the jack-o'-lantern's lid and spotted the little bit of green inside. "Some joker put this in." I pulled out the dried four-leaf clover and then fitted the lid back on the pumpkin. When I waved my hand in front of the jack-o'-lantern, it began saying, "Boo-boo-boo," like it was trying to get rid of a year's worth of "Boos" in one minute.

"It still doesn't sound very scary," Saskia said.

"But at least it's saying the right thing." Mabli erased an item from the list on her phone. "So that's one more thing down, and fifty thousand to go."

At that moment, one of the auditorium doors opened, knocking into me. "Oh, just the person we wanted to see," said Lupe, passing through. Then came Nanette and Ms. Kululu. As a precaution, our teacher now carried her textbook with her at all times.

"Winnie, will you be my assistant in my magical act?" Nanette asked.

I smelled a setup for something. "I thought Lupe was going to help you," I said.

"Lupe's shy." Nanette nudged Lupe. "Aren't you, Lupe?"

"Yeah, real shy." Lupe nodded.

I shook my head. "Sorry. The decorating committee's got too much to do."

"Look," Nanette said to me. "I know I got off on the wrong foot with you, and I'd like to make up for that. My aunt may not get along with Miss Drake, but that doesn't mean we have to be enemies. Tell you what. I'll call you when I'm ready to rehearse. That way you can work with your committee before and after we practice."

I didn't care if I looked like a sorehead. "No can do."

Nanette turned to Ms. Kululu. "We thought that might be the case, so we checked with Ms. Kululu first." Ms. Kululu was the faculty adviser in charge of the decorating committee, but up until now, she'd left us alone.

"Performing at the Festival is a great honor, so I think it's a very generous gesture on Nanette's part," Ms. Kululu said. "But of course, the decision is up to you, Winnie."

I was still going to refuse, but Mabli touched my arm and whispered in my ear. "You'll look bad if you don't do it," she said. "I'll make sure one of us keeps an eye on you during the rehearsals."

I felt like I was boxed in. "Well, let's try it."

"Great," Nanette said, and waved for me. "It's just about our turn."

We went into the auditorium to wait near the stage. Leslie, a second-year middle school witch, was finishing her rehearsal. She'd just tossed a pitcher of water up high and was making the column of water slide through the air in various shapes. Then, as "Monster Mash" began to play, she made the water spread out into a mist that became various monsters, each one more ghoulish or funnier than the last.

True to her word, Mabli stood in front of the stage with Ms. Kululu, so I began to feel more confident.

And my rehearsal with Nanette wasn't bad. She was

rather patient putting me on my various marks and explaining what I had to do for each trick. The tricks themselves were the standard ones but with a little twist—like having little top hats come out of a rabbit's ear.

So I stopped worrying—and stepped onto the bull's-eye where Nanette wanted me.

⌒⌒ MISS DRAKE ⌒⌒

The next morning, I fussed over my disguise as the human Miss Drake, because Liza had invited me for coffee and pastry. As I was giving myself one last inspection in the mirror, I got a text message from Reynard.

R: Jarvis's goons refuse 2 go back 2 yur house.

D: Has he fired them? Will he bring in new team?

R: Don't know. Maybe. 4 now, goons 2 just watch
yur house & school @ a distance.

That was reassuring in a way. At least, they wouldn't spoil Halloween for Winnie.

I left my apartment by my back door, walked through the park, back to our house, so Liza wouldn't be aware I was living downstairs.

When Liza opened the door, she greeted me. "Thank you for coming on such short notice, Miss Drake."

"I'm always happy to see you," I said. "How is your job?"

"Rhiannon couldn't be a better boss," Liza said. "She understood when I told her I'd be coming in a little late this morning."

She led me into the living room, where fruit tarts and tea had been laid out on the coffee table.

Liza smiled as she saw me looking through the window. Pulling in her shoulders, she gave a little shiver of delight. "I love this room. Such a beautiful view and so much light."

"And such good company," I agreed.

Liza poured my coffee, and I selected one of Vasilisa's delicious tarts. We'd met like this before, and I'd always found Liza pleasant company. But today she seemed on edge.

Liza immediately got around to the point of inviting me this morning. "You were good friends with Aunt Amelia. Did you go to Spriggs too?"

"No, I never had that privilege," I said.

Liza looked disappointed. "How well do you know the Academy?"

"I know it has an excellent reputation," I answered.

"Do you know any more of its graduates?" she asked. Since Liza had promised Winnie not to talk openly about magicals, she was dancing all around the topic instead to see if I already knew about them.

"I know quite a few," I said. "They all have excellent characters. Spriggs will do right by Winnie."

Poor Liza definitely wanted to know about magicals. She looked ready to burst with questions. "But did you ever notice anything . . . different about any of them?"

"Everyone is unique," I said. "Spriggs is particularly good at helping its students appreciate their uniqueness."

"Umm, unique." Liza chewed on that word and then leaned forward so that she was sitting on the very edge of the sofa cushion. "But do you think Winnie is safe there?"

Ah, you're afraid of what the magicals might do to Winnie.

"She's as safe as she could be at home," I assured her, and added, "perhaps even safer."

Clearly, Liza was worried about the school. I kept my claws crossed that the Festival would ease some of her fears.

Early Halloween evening, as I gave a last-minute adjustment to my costume, I heard cloth rustling behind me. Hanging from the top rail of a chair was a bag with intricate lace patterns on its sides. It was swaying back and forth as if in a wind—even though the air was calm in the room.

The bag was a gift from my friend Sefa Bubbles. The sack usually forgot what it had inside it, but it often provided something useful. Though I couldn't pin down the reason, some presentiment made me take it. Even if we didn't need it, a witch's bag might also want to go out on Halloween too. Then I hurried through my back door. Around me, I felt a dozen furry and feathered friends keeping watch.

I felt more friendly eyes following me as I walked back to our house. Everyone was on high alert tonight.

Vasilisa was already handing out candy from a bowl to some trick-or-treaters.

There were big red spots of rouge on her cheeks, and she wore a bandana and dress like her doll. "Good evening, Miss Drake," she said as I slipped around the visitors and into the house.

Winnie ran out of the living room. The makeup on her face made her look pale as a ghost, and she was wearing a tattered shawl over a ragged dress. She pirouetted. "We got my stuff from a thrift store, and then Mom cut it up and altered it for me. What do you think?"

I complimented her. "You make a very pretty ghost."

"Not just any ghost." Winnie tapped the necklace of shells around her neck. "I'm Molly Malone's ghost."

"She had a wheelbarrow, but that would be a bit cumbersome." I thought I understood now why Sefa Bubbles's bag had insisted on coming along. "Take this and hang the shells from it so you'll look like you're selling them."

No sooner had Winnie hung the necklace half in and half out of the bag than a large sign appeared on the string of shells: COCKLES AND MUSSELS CHEAP.

"Perfect," she said, delighted. "Thank you, magic bag."

Sefa's bag of tricks had helped us before, and as Winnie slung the bag onto her shoulder, I asked, "How about my outfit?"

She examined me from all angles. "Great dragon costume, Miss Drake," she said with a wink. Except for the big zipper down the back, it wasn't much different from my normal look. I had it special-ordered from Clipper's Emporium.

Liza came from the living room in a tasteful black dress that Sefa Bubbles would have approved.

"And you look very fetching for a witch," I said.

"Thank you, but how did you even know I was one?" Liza gestured at her outfit. "When we made our costumes, Winnie insisted that I not wear a pointy hat."

Well done, Winnie. You just saved your mother from an embarrassing faux pas.

"I understand they're out of fashion now," I said politely.

Winnie's tongue stuck out slightly from the corner of her mouth as she dug around in Sefa's bag. Suddenly she grinned. "Here, Mom. This will finish your outfit." She lifted a pair of earrings on which silver crescent moons and alchemical symbols dangled.

"Why, thank you, Winnie," Liza said.

I saw Liza studying me intently, perhaps wondering if I was a magical.

I'd prepared my disguise for just this eventuality. "I'm afraid I only bought mine."

I turned so Liza could see the zipper down my back. Then I took off my dragon mask to reveal my regular human disguise.

Liza looked reassured that I seemed a natural like her. "It's very good."

While we had been inspecting one another's costumes, Vasilisa had been handing out candy to more trick-or-treaters, but finally there was a lull. As she set the bowl down on a small table, Liza glanced at the contents.

"I would have sworn I put in a bag of little chocolate bars," she said.

"They were very popular," Vasilisa said. I was sure they had met with Small Doll's approval.

I wondered what would happen to the trick-or-treaters who came calling on us tonight. Would Vasilisa's doll take the chocolate from their bags too? I was afraid that our visitors might find more *trick* than *treat* at our house.

Liza, Winnie, and I admired the Halloween decorations as we strolled toward Spriggs. Some houses had gone all out, with ghosts and witches flitting about on pulleys while speakers played spooky music. One mansion even had transformed its lawn into a cemetery with ghosts and ghouls peeking out from behind fake tombstones.

The sidewalks were swarming with costumed children and their parents. None of the naturals knew that the vampire next to them might be real. Halloween was the one night when magical families did not have to disguise themselves as humans but could walk the streets as themselves.

Winnie was almost squirming with excitement. "Wait till you see what we've done to the auditorium."

I remembered the morning of her first day at Spriggs. Then she had spoken anxiously about the magicals. Now it was *we*. Perhaps Winnie was fitting in with the other students, because she was magical in her own way.

When we got inside, we found Zaina, Mabli, and Liri waiting with their families. Zaina was dressed as a doctor, while Mabli was wearing a pilot's uniform. Liri was wearing some kind of superhero costume.

Liza tried her best not to stare as introductions were made all around, and the magical families were doing their best to make her feel comfortable.

Liri's parents wore uniforms like the Union soldiers from the American Civil War. Liri's mother had the epaulets of a general, while her father was a mere private.

Liri's mother slipped her arm through Liza's. "Some days, your daughter is all Liri talks about. Winnie did this and Winnie did that."

Liza groaned in alarm. "Oh no, what did Winnie do?"

Liri's mother gave a bubbling laugh, and silvery pearl-size bubbles floated upward through her throat. "Don't worry. They were all good things."

"And this is my little sister, Megan," Liri said. "She's eight."

Her costume seemed to be piles of green leaves, so I asked, "Are you supposed to be a salad?"

Megan rolled her eyes as if my IQ had gone down in her opinion.

Liri was more polite, simply nodding to her sister's pointed ears. "Megan is an elf."

Clearly, she should have shopped for her costume at Clipper's.

Charlemagne in all his glory would have envied the costumes of Mabli's parents. They were both dressed sumptuously like medieval royalty in rich velvet and satin outfits with fake fur trimming. Their gold necklaces and diamond jewelry, though, were very real.

Mabli's mother reached up and patted Liza's arm reassuringly. "We know this is all new to you, dear, so if you have any questions, feel free to ask."

"I'm just afraid I'm going to offend someone," Liza confessed.

"You leave them to us," Mabli's father assured her.

Winnie grabbed her mother's hand. "Come see, come see."

As Winnie eagerly led her mother, I fell into step with the others. "I want to thank you for being so kind and understanding to Liza."

"We love Winnie," Zaina's mother said, "and we're sure we'll love Liza too."

Winnie was hopping first on one foot and then the other as she waited by the doors that led down to the auditorium. A large pumpkin next to them was barking, "Boo-boo-boo."

"Hurry," Winnie said, waving her free hand.

When we were all next to her, she said, "Ta-da!" Then she and Mabli opened both doors. "This way to the Magical Wonders of the World!"

CHAPTER TEN

Flaws are what other pets have.
Your pet's eccentricities are signs of character.

Winnie

Mom stared at the mouth of the glowing green tunnel that filled most of the doorway. "What is this?"

"The northern lights," I explained. "The science club gathered some of them and made them into a slide."

"Your science club did all this?" Mom asked in amazement.

"Well, our science teacher, Sir Isaac, advised them," I admitted.

"Sir Isaac?" Mom asked. "You have British nobility too?"

I thought Mom had more than enough to handle at the moment, so I tugged at her arm. "Come on, Mom. Do you want to talk about the teachers or do you want to have fun?"

Mom pointed at the side where the usual stairs still showed. "I think I'd rather use the steps instead. Awk!"

Mom waved her arms as she fell into the tunnel, leaving wide stripes of sparkling green behind her as she disappeared.

I looked over my shoulder at Miss Drake, who quickly tucked her paws behind her. "Oops, how clumsy of me."

I threw myself headfirst down the soft-sided tunnel, sparks flying as I flew by.

"Mom, are you okay?" I shouted.

"Woo-hoo!" Mom screamed back. "This is better than a roller coaster!"

Mom and I landed with a *whump* in a six-foot-tall pile of moss. We sank into it, the earthy smell filling our noses.

I heard a whooshing sound as something barreled down the tunnel. Miss Drake shot out hind paws first, but instead of falling into the moss, she drew in her legs and tumbled across it like a ball. She came to a clean stop—like she'd been landing on a thick bed of moss all her life.

Standing up, she began brushing herself off. "Most entertaining."

"Show-off," I muttered.

"I see no reason to hide my candle under a bushel basket."

She pulled Mom and me to our feet, and we high-stepped through the spongy moss toward one of the little doors on the side of the pit. Then we waited until all my friends joined us.

The tables in the cafeteria-auditorium were gone. In their place, booths had been set up, and the ceiling and walls pushed into other dimensions to form a giant cavern.

Mom's eyes grew as big as saucers, and her mouth opened in a little O. While I'd been doing and seeing so many wonderful things with Miss Drake, it had been hard not to share them with Mom. Now I had a chance to show her some of the magic.

"Let's try one of the magical wonders," I said, taking her hand and leading her. "We learned all about Colossus of Kush in magic class. The real one was a quarter-mile high. A powerful wizard made spirits carve it out of a hill, Jibal et Tarabel, in just one night."

Mom craned her neck back, looking at the huge thirty-foot statue of a man in a kilt and a bullet-shaped hat. Several kids were climbing up the pegs set into the sides.

"Shouldn't they be wearing safety harnesses?" Mom asked.

One of the girls in a mountain climbing club sweatshirt came over. "They're all wearing charms, ma'am. Our faculty adviser especially made them." She pointed to a snowflake design made of straw. "You can't fall with one of these."

Mom frowned. "That looks pretty flimsy to me."

There was a cry from above as a girl lost her grip on a peg. She laughed as she floated in midair till she could grab some pegs and climb again.

"See? It's perfectly safe," the club member assured her.

"We'll show you," Mabli said, tilting her face and slipping the charm's ribbon over her head. Then, setting her feet on the lowest pegs, Mabli reached for higher ones and began to climb. "Race you," Mabli called to us.

With her short arms and legs, that seemed like a silly dare.

As the club member put a charm on Mom and me, I said, "Let's race."

Mom still looked doubtful. "I'd feel better with real harnesses around us instead of something that looks like a Christmas ornament," she insisted.

"The charms will work just as well because magic *is* real, Liza," Miss Drake said. "That's what Winnie is trying to show you. Let her."

"Please, Mom, please," I begged.

"I must be crazy," Mom muttered, but she began climbing with me.

Liri and I went up next, but Zaina and her family waited until we were halfway up before they started. Since their bodies were half air, they zipped up the colossus's side past us. Mom was grinning as we worked our way back down. "Okay, I'll admit that was fun."

"Let's cool off over there." I pointed into the big pool of water the marine biology club had set up. In it was a scaled-down temple of living coral. Anemones clung to the walls like flowers. Giant sponges filled niches like statues of naiads, merpeople, and sea creatures.

"More magic?" Mom asked.

I grinned. "Yeah, isn't it great? Instant indoor pool."

"My ancestors built the real Temple of Amphitrite in the Aegean Sea," Liri boasted. "It was as big as the island of Crete."

"But this one has a fun game inside." A club member

offered us charms to let us breathe underwater and keep us dry. Each charm was a seaweed leaf cut into the shape of a sea horse and had a spell written in Chinese characters on it.

"I'd do this only for you, Winnie," Mom said as she put the charm in her pocket. Holding her nose, she jumped.

I swam over to where Mom was floating, her cheeks bulging like a chipmunk's.

"It's okay, Mom," I encouraged her. "We can breathe and talk."

"Amazing," Mom said. I heard the word like I had a wet towel over my ears.

With a sudden kick, she did a backflip. "I could get to like this." Then she started doing acrobatic tricks.

Caught up in the spirit of the Festival now, Mom talked us into a race on magical carpets. She whizzed past all of us and came in first. Everyone congratulated her, and she looked really happy and, even better, comfortable at last.

While Miss Drake and I stopped to get lemonade, Mom left and brought back three school pendants, one for each of us. "So we'll remember tonight."

"Thank you," Miss Drake said politely. "I'll always treasure this."

"So you're glad you let me go to Spriggs?" I asked Mom.

"It's an incredible place," Mom said.

"I wouldn't trade my friends or the Academy for anything," I told her.

Mom hesitated, then spoke the words I wanted to hear. "I wouldn't ask you to."

"Thanks, Mom," I said, and gave her a hug. "And you're not mad anymore about my keeping quiet about stuff?"

"You're still not completely out of the doghouse yet." Mom laughed. "But right now my mind is officially overloaded with impossible things."

"You're doing very well, Liza," Miss Drake said.

Mom gazed at Miss Drake thoughtfully. "And just who are *you*, Miss Drake?"

I held my breath, but I should have trusted how slippery Miss Drake could be with words.

"Liza, I'm your friend," she said, "and I would never let anything bad happen to Winnie."

"I guess that'll do for now," said Mom.

As I was sighing in relief, Nanette came over. She was wearing a blue satin dress and a black cape with the moon and the stars sewn in silver thread. A silver chain circled her head, and a veil hung from it down her back.

"Good evening, Miss Drake." Nanette curtsied to her and then to Mom. "And you must be Winnie's mother. I'm Nanette Cellini."

"Hi," Mom said.

Nanette turned and motioned to the man behind her. "And this is my father, Mr. Cellini."

Mr. Cellini had a neatly cut brown beard. His pirate costume looked tailored and very expensive.

"And this is my aunt Silana Voisin." Nanette motioned to the woman next to her father. She wore a long purple velvet gown and a tiara with diamonds that sparkled like the lights on a theater marquee.

"What a lovely tiara, Silana," Miss Drake said.

Silana touched her fingertips to it. "Yes, tiaras are so much better custom-designed than the gaudy prizes one wins in a contest, don't you think?"

Miss Drake beat Silana every year in the magic contest at the Enchanters' Fair, and each time won a tiara. By now, Miss Drake had a trunkful, and none of them looked gaudy to me.

"I wouldn't know," Miss Drake reminded her. "I never had any need to have one made."

I thought I heard Silana grinding her teeth together, but Nanette defended her aunt. "My aunt's the best sorceress in all of San Francisco. She's taught me everything I know."

"Nanette gets all her talent from her mother," Mr. Cellini confessed. "I'm only good at making money, not magic."

Nanette pointed to Sefa Bubbles's bag on my shoulder. "Leave that. It's time for us to go on."

When we'd rehearsed her magic act, only a few people had been watching. Now our audience would fill the auditorium. I stroked the bag's strap. Just touching it made me feel calmer. "It's part of my costume."

Nanette frowned, but then she simply shrugged. "Suit yourself."

A few feet away, Lupe was smirking. What did the two of them have up their sleeves?

I touched Sefa Bubbles's bag again. At least I had this—and Miss Drake would not be far away if I needed her.

ᜈ MISS DRAKE ᜈ

As Winnie walked away with Nanette, I asked Winnie's friends, "What's going on?"

But it was Silana who answered smugly, "Oh, didn't you hear? My niece graciously invited Winnie to perform with her."

I felt my spine turn to ice down to the tip of my tail. I had been so busy with outside threats that I hadn't worried about homegrown ones. I leaned in close to Silana and growled. "You've done some pretty low things, Silana, but striking at me through Winnie is the lowest."

"Don't be absurd." Silana dismissed me. "A Festival is for fun, not for feuding."

"Shall we?" Mr. Cellini asked Liza, and together with almost all of Winnie's friends and their families, they moved toward the stage.

Only Mabli hung back to whisper to me, "Don't worry. We've kept an eye on the rehearsals, and it's just a regular magic act."

I still had my doubts as we joined the others, and more festivalgoers crowded in behind.

When Mr. Cellini slipped on a pair of glasses, Silana looked at him oddly. "When did you start wearing glasses?"

"Just a few days ago," Mr. Cellini said as the lights began to dim.

When the curtain opened, Nanette was standing before an eight-foot-high pillar—another magical wonder, the Pillar of Night. Its sides were of black crystal, and a cloud of stars whirled over it. She raised her hand dramatically, and the stars spiraled into the pillar like water going down a drain. Then the pillar shrank and suddenly flew into Nanette's hand.

"By Amphitrite and Eurybia," Nanette announced loudly, "I summon thee."

The next moment, a huge sea turtle paddled leisurely in midair over the stage.

"Huh," Zaina said. "That's new."

Suddenly, Mabli looked worried. "Yeah."

"I don't think Nanette plans to do the tricks she rehearsed," Zaina said. "She fooled us."

As Nanette bowed to the audience's applause, Winnie stumbled out of the wings—I was willing to bet that Lupe had shoved her onto the stage. Sefa's bag hung from one shoulder, making it awkward for Winnie to carry the crystal ball in her hands.

Whipping around, Nanette pointed her wand at the sea turtle. It shot across the stage toward Winnie.

As soon as she saw it coming, though, Winnie dropped the ball, which began to roll across the boards. The next instant, her hand dipped into the bag, and she pulled out . . . a pink parasol. She barely had time to open it before Nanette stabbed the wand at the air. A second later and the sea turtle burst like a balloon—one full of blue paint.

The paint covered the stage and the parasol but not Winnie. Nanette shrugged and waved her wand. The paint turned into turquoise butterflies, fluttering up to the ceiling.

Winnie shook off the last of the butterflies from the parasol, closed it, and put it back into the bag. Though the parasol was much longer than the bag, it disappeared inside.

Assuming this was the end of the trick, people began to clap enthusiastically. Liri cupped her hands around her mouth. "Take a bow, Winnie!" she shouted.

Winnie hesitated, then dipped her head.

As Nanette glared, I saw the family resemblance to her aunt. Silana looked daggers at me just like that each time I beat her at the magic contest.

Winnie kept bowing while backing offstage, but Nanette was finishing the next spell.

Worried, I asked Mabli, "What's supposed to happen next?"

It was Zaina who spoke first. "Well, Nanette should make the crystal ball fly around."

But the ball began to expand instead, swelling larger and larger until it became a bubble floating through the air toward Winnie. As she stood there in surprise, it dropped over her, swallowing her with a loud *POP*.

"Catch," Nanette called to the audience, and waved her hand. That puff of air was enough to make the bubble change direction toward the lip of the stage. Inside the ball, Winnie tried to trot to stay upright but tripped instead and fell.

Lupe had come around and was standing in the front row to our right. She caught the bubble without breaking it and tossed it and Winnie into the audience as if they were both light as feathers. Inside the bubble, Winnie tumbled awkwardly.

I was just about to give up on keeping my identity secret from Liza and fly after her daughter, when Winnie managed to get to her knees.

By now, she was ten feet from the stage, where the audience was slowly passing her from one to another, but they stopped when Winnie held up her hands. I could see her looking around for me, but before I could even wave to get her attention, she looked down at where Sefa's bag had fallen to the bottom of the bubble.

She took out a tiny globe of the world, then a doll's pillow and an orange. She tossed them one, two, three into the air and began to juggle—a handy skill her father had taught her.

As the audience started to applaud, Nanette shouted, annoyed, "Keep the bubble moving."

Before people could start handing the bubble around, though, gold foil-wrapped candies began to pour out of Sefa's bag.

A woman peered up at the bubble. "Hey, that candy sells for fifty dollars a pound."

Dropping her juggling items, Winnie raised Sefa's bag with both hands and turned it upside down until there was enough candy to hide her shins before the flow of sweets stopped.

As children and adults eagerly pressed in closer, I thought it was too bad Small Doll wasn't here.

Moving her free arm in a grand sweep, Winnie dipped her hand into the sack and rummaged around for a bit before she pulled out a long knitting needle. With the palm of her free hand, she motioned to the needle. I could hear her call in a loud and steady voice: "Happy Halloween, everyone!"

With one last flourish of the needle, she punctured the sphere.

The magic bubble burst, and Winnie and the candy fell onto the audience. As the children scrambled to get the candy, I saw Winnie in the arms of a man in a red Beefeater's costume.

"A most artful trick, Burton," Sir Isaac declared as he set her on her feet.

I had to agree. Sefa's bag was outdoing itself.

The members of the audience who weren't bending over for the candy began to clap.

Onstage, Nanette had turned an interesting shade of red, but she forced herself to smile. "Let's finish the act, Winnie."

Slipping the knitting needle back into the bag, Winnie grabbed the lip of the stage and climbed back up.

Too late, I saw Nanette finish moving her wand in a mystical sign unfamiliar to me. She must have been working an enchantment while we had all been distracted.

Silana shook her head as she murmured, "Are you crazy, Nanette?"

At that same moment, Nanette snatched off her cape and flung it into the air toward Winnie. "Evanesce!"

The cape began to ripple, stretching and stretching until it looked like a dark flood some fifteen feet across. The moon and stars on it no longer seemed like decorations but the real thing, and the cape reminded me of a spider hunting for something . . . or someone.

Desperately, Winnie reached into her bag and pulled out . . . a Ping-Pong paddle.

That stupid bag!

Winnie swung the paddle at the cape, perhaps trying to knock the edge away from her.

Instead, though, the cape bounced backward like a rubber ball.

Hmm, maybe the bag isn't as forgetful as I thought. Perhaps it has a sense of humor.

When the cape hit the back wall, it bounded forward again.

And over Nanette.

She crouched, holding her hands up over her head. "No, go away!"

But the cape settled around her so that we could see her shape beneath the cloth. Frantic, Silana was trying to pull herself up onstage.

It was strange, but the cape kept descending. And beneath it, Nanette's shape kept shrinking until the cape was lying flat on the wooden floor.

Silana dragged the huge cape over the stage to her, clutching fold after fold against her, but there were now just the bare boards where Nanette had been.

Behind her, Winnie's free hand was searching desperately in Sefa's bag. She wrinkled her forehead in puzzlement as she felt around. When she pulled out a note, she read it and then held it up as she walked over to Silana. "This says I should hit the cape with the paddle again. May I?"

Dazed, Silana gave the bunched-up cape to Winnie. Winnie tapped the paddle against it.

"Why isn't something happening?" a worried Mr. Cellini demanded.

I surged onto the stage and over to Winnie. "I think when the cape isn't in the air," I whispered, "the paddle just treats it like it's cloth. So I'll toss the cape into the air, and then you hit it."

Winnie gripped the paddle handle in both hands. "Ready."

I threw the cape into the air over an empty part of the stage. It kept spreading and rippling outward like a dark pool again. Winnie stepped over, careful to avoid being beneath it, and swung at the edge. She hit it so hard this time that the cape shot against the rear wall and ricocheted off.

I grabbed Winnie's shoulders and pulled her backward out of its path. Silana scrambled over by us, watching with everyone else as the cape hit the stage.

"Ow!" Nanette cried.

As the cape bounced upward again, it left behind a stunned and bedraggled Nanette, wand still in one hand.

Silana dragged her niece to a safe spot on the side, and then snatched the wand from Nanette's fingers. As the cape bounded about, Silana worked a spell. When she finished, the cape suddenly hovered in the air and began to shrink until it was back to its normal size.

Then it plopped to the floor, a harmless piece of clothing again.

I heard Mabli whistle. "Good one, Winnie."

The applause was thunderous. I could barely hear Winnie say to me, "But Sefa's bag did all the work."

I took her hand and led her forward. "Take a bow anyway."

When we did, the clapping got even louder. As we straightened, I felt Silana take my hand. "I didn't teach her that spell to use on anyone. You have to believe me."

Her eyes pleaded with me for mercy. We had to make it seem like we had planned the whole thing or her niece would be in big trouble. Nanette might get by with detention for playing a prank with the paint or the ball, but deliberately trying to make a fellow student vanish could mean expulsion and no recommendation to any decent school.

I leaned forward slightly to see that Silana's other hand gripped Nanette's. With a nod, I stepped forward and so did Winnie and a grateful Silana. A dazed Nanette stumbled along.

And then we bowed together.

* * *

Mortimer, the gargoyle on the gate, was watching out for threats to the school grounds, and not family quarrels. So the gatekeeper merely observed Nanette snatch the glasses from her father's nose.

"Take off these stupid things," she growled.

Mr. Cellini tried to grab them from her. "That camera's a very expensive prototype."

"I don't want to remember tonight ever, and I certainly don't want to see a movie of it!" Nanette brought her shoe down hard on the glasses, and they broke with a loud crack.

"What are you talking about, Nanette?" Silana demanded.

Mr. Cellini stared down angrily at the broken glasses. "That was an experimental video camera that can store up to a hundred films in the glasses' arms."

"It's strictly forbidden to record the Festival in any form," Silana said, and for a moment, the air turned as freezing as an Arctic night. Even though he was stone, the gargoyle shivered. "After I finish talking to your father, my dear niece, I'm going to review when it's proper to use attack spells and when you shouldn't."

"It was all Winnie's fault," Nanette argued. "She kept stealing my applause."

"And a good thing she did," Mr. Cellini said, "or who knows where you'd be now."

The three were still arguing as they got into a car and drove off.

Being iron, Mortimer didn't know about dandruff so he didn't know the name of the little white flakes dusting the natural's shoulders. But as the natural retrieved the pieces of the glasses and put them into his coat pocket, Mortimer thought it was nice that he had picked up the others' litter. *There's still some hope for naturals after all,* the gatekeeper thought.

Mortimer only repeated the incident much later when I interrogated the gargoyles as I tried to understand what had happened. If only I had spoken to him that night, I could have headed off so much trouble later.

CHAPTER ELEVEN

Nothing annoys your enemies so much as forgiving them.

∽ Winnie ∽

The day after Halloween, I was rushing up the stairs, hoping to make it to school on time. I had forgotten to round up my overdue library books. My backpack was stuffed, my arms were loaded too, and I was late. Luckily, Mabli saw me and swung the main door open just in time.

"Your ears must be ringing," she said as I slipped by.

"Not a bit," I said as I hurried toward my locker. "Why?"

Mabli caught a library book that slipped out of my backpack. "Everyone is talking about you . . . you and Nanette and your magic show."

"I'd like to forget the whole thing," I told her. "No chance, huh?"

"No way," she said. "You two are the talk of the school."

I crammed my stuff in my locker and got my English books.

Everyone I met on the way to homeroom had questions. Was I afraid? *(At times.)*

How did I know what to do? *(I didn't, but my bag did.)*

Where did I learn magic? *(Again, the bag was magic. I just reached in, got something out, and tried to figure out how to use it.)*

Whose bag was it? *(A very clever witch to whom I was very, very grateful.)*

Where did I get it? *(Borrowed from a friend to whom I was even more grateful.)*

Down the hallway, I saw Nanette. Or rather, I felt her eyes burning into my back, and turned to face her.

If looks could kill, she would have gotten her wish then and there.

Most of the girls were avoiding her like she stunk of old fish and rotted vegetables. My guess is that she had broken a Spriggs code or two last night. As she walked down the hall, girls moved aside, pressing their backs against their lockers.

"I have nothing to say to you," she grumbled as she passed me. Her face was pale and stonelike.

"Back at you," I called after her.

But when we settled into our first class, her seat was empty.

"Nanette got called to Ms. Griffin's office," Mabli whispered to me. "I'm glad I'm not her right now. The principal wants to know why the tricks she did in rehearsals didn't match the ones at the Festival."

Nanette wasn't in our other morning classes either. In between, the chatter was all about whether she would be suspended or expelled or given some nasty punishment.

How about ordering her to write *I will not make my fellow classmate disappear* three trillion times. That would keep her out of my way for a while.

Sir Isaac was the teacher on duty during lunch. He tapped me on the shoulder. "Burton, report to Ms. Griffin's office immediately."

"But I haven't done anything," I protested.

He flapped his hands like tiny wings. "Fly, Burton, fly. She's not in the best temper today."

All I'd done the other night was protect myself from a crazy classmate and her magic. I was getting my defense arguments together, but they vanished when I entered the office.

Nanette sat in front of Ms. Griffin, and it looked like she had been crying.

Ms. Griffin folded her hands on her desk. "Nanette said that she changed the approved program to a more exciting and potentially dangerous one at the last moment. Did she warn you in advance?"

"No, ma'am," I said.

"That's what she also said. So I had Nanette write an apology to you," Ms. Griffin said.

Nanette passed one of her fancy personal note cards to me, and I read:

Dear Winnie,
At the Festival, I wanted to show off and show you up.
I didn't think about how you could have been hurt.

I'M SORRY.
Nanette

I didn't want to be there any more than she did. I put the card in my pocket to tear up later. "Apology accepted. Are we done?"

Nanette drew her eyebrows together angrily. "That's all you've got to say back to me? I had to sit here all morning thinking about what I did and what could have happened. What about all the stuff you've done to me?"

I could feel myself getting mad too. "I'm not going to apologize for turning the tables on you at the Festival."

Her grudges started to spill out of her. "It's your fault I went too far. You hogged the spotlight and made me angry. Before that, you were always topping me—like with Nessie. I had the best question. All you did was ask her to sing, but Lady Louhi made a fuss over you."

I stared at her, amazed, and annoyed too. "I'm only trying to get through school like everyone else. You're the last thing I'd want to think about."

Nanette's pen just missed me when she threw it. "The only thing worse than losing a contest is losing it to someone who isn't even trying to win."

"Enough!" Ms. Griffin snapped. When our principal used that tone, no one argued, and when she spoke, the words marched from her mouth like soldiers carrying a coffin. "I wanted you girls to bury the hatchet—but not in each other! We have to resolve this issue before someone gets hurt. Most conflicts start because people fail to understand one another. So, starting today and for the rest of the week, you will spend all your time together while you are in school."

"What?" I asked, shocked.

Almost at the same time, Nanette said, "That's ridiculous."

Ms. Griffin held up a hand, and I realized it was going to get worse. "In that time, I want you both to get to know one another and find some way to get along."

"Why do I have to keep being punished?" Nanette protested. "I said I was sorry."

"Hey, now I'm the one being punished," I complained.

"Make that two weeks together!" Ms. Griffin said sharply. She glanced back and forth, waiting for either of us to object. When we both kept our mouths shut this time, she added ominously, "And if you haven't been able to reach an agreement by the end of that period, I will take even more drastic steps."

Even Miss Drake couldn't find a bright side to my situation. I think she was imagining being glued to Silana.

"This is going to be a looong two weeks," she told me.

And it was, starting with the next day. All our teachers began to adapt their lessons around our punishment— but it felt like they were ganging up on us. Sir Isaac called it another "learning experience," so we studied magnets. Opposites attracted, but two magnets with the same polarity repulsed one another.

"No way are we the same," Nanette muttered, and for once I agreed with her.

The day after that, Ms. Kululu had the class write a hundred-word autobiography and then exchange it with the person next to us. Of course, I got Nanette's, and she got mine.

I expected her autobiography to brag about all the stuff she owned and the fancy vacations she took. But it was very short and simple.

I kept my voice low when I finished hers and handed it back. "I'm sorry about your mom. No one knows what happened to her?"

Nanette's Mom was/had been a sorceress like her sister, Silana Voisin.

"One day she was working in her room. . . ." Nanette closed her hand into a fist and then spread her fingers out in an explosion. "And the next, poof! She was gone in a flash of light."

"Doesn't that scare you about sorcery?" I asked.

Nanette pointed at my autobiography. "You said your mom fell off a horse and got hurt. Does that scare you about horses?"

"No," I said. "Riding's too much a part of me."

"Same with sorcery. It's in my blood." She massaged her palm. "I'm . . . I'm sorry about your dad. Do you miss him?"

"Every day when I wake up and realize he's gone, it hurts all over again," I admitted. It looked like we had something in common, but then Nanette had to turn even misery into a competition.

"It's worse for me," she said. "At least you know he's gone, but I don't know if my mom is alive or dead. The hoping just draws out the ache."

I rolled my eyes. I started counting the hours and minutes left of our punishment. Too many . . . way too many!

But it wasn't until PE class that I began to understand Nanette better. Ms. Gideon, our teacher, decided to have races with two-person relay teams. I think the idea was for Nanette and me to learn to work together.

Each runner made a circuit of the gym marked by small orange cones. We weren't going to do anything fancy like passing on batons. The first runner just had to tag the second.

I knew something about racehorses from Mom's time

in the stables. "I think I've got a better burst of speed in the beginning," I explained, "but then I start to fade. But you get faster as you run. So why don't I go first and maybe get us a lead and you run the anchor?"

"No one will beat me." Nanette eyed me. "Just don't stumble over your two left feet."

We actually did pretty well until the semifinal heat. We were up against Saskia and Kari, and Saskia was the fastest person in our class. As part centaur, I think she was part racehorse.

The gym echoed with the encouraging shouts and clapping from my friends, but though I tried my best, Saskia pulled ahead of me. By the time I tagged Nanette, Kari was long gone.

"It's about time," Nanette snarled.

The cords and muscles on her neck stood out as she strained to catch up with Kari. I didn't think Nanette could keep it up, but bit by bit she edged closer. Then Kari faltered, and that let Nanette shoot ahead. I thought that she would ease up then, but she didn't.

"Come on, Kari," Saskia hollered. "Get the lead out."

Kari started to run faster again, but the gap was too big. Yet just as she neared the finish line, Nanette stumbled and reached down for her calf. Her face twisted in pain, as she fell and scraped her knee too.

I started for her at the same time as Ms. Gideon. I thought for sure Nanette would stop, but though she could barely limp, she crossed the line just ahead of Kari.

"Sit down so I can check that leg, Cellini," Ms. Gideon said.

"Let me help." I put an arm around Nanette and helped lower her to the floor. Her T-shirt was soaked with sweat from her effort.

As Ms. Gideon felt her ankle and calf, Nanette said, "I just got a cramp. If you just wait until I can walk it off, I can keep on running."

Ms. Gideon shook her head. "It's more important to get some fluid into you, Cellini. Burton, help Cellini to the water fountain and then ask the nurse to bandage that floor burn. Since there won't be time to change out of your shorts and T-shirt, I'll have someone get your uniforms from your gym lockers and give them to you in your next class. You'll need to change in a restroom later."

As Ms. Gideon headed back toward the rest of the class, Nanette held out an arm toward me. "Help me up," she whispered fiercely.

I wasn't sure her leg would hold steady. "Rest a few more minutes."

"Help me up!" Nanette insisted.

So I got an arm around her and aided her in getting up to her feet. She began to stamp around as if she could drive the cramp from her leg. "We're ready, Ms. Gideon," she called, though she was still limping.

"You most definitely *are* not." Ms. Gideon glanced at her watch. "Anyway, class is almost over."

"You can't do this to me!" Nanette protested.

But Ms. Gideon ignored her. "Zaina and Liri win!"

As the others let out a cheer, I watched in surprise as a tear streaked down Nanette's cheek.

I repeated what my mom had taught me. "Hey, don't feel bad. We tried our best."

She shoved me away. "Trying's not good enough. You're the best, or you're nothing."

When she began to wobble, I put my arm around her. "Who told you that? Your dad?"

"No, my aunt," Nanette said as we left the gym. "But he'd agree with her."

When I'd first met Nanette, I thought she looked down on everyone. But maybe it was more like she needed to be better than everyone else because she was trying to please her aunt, her dad, and herself. "Nobody's perfect all the time."

"I have to be the best if I'm going to find my mom one day," Nanette insisted. "That's always my goal."

I guess if I had a chance to bring back Dad, I'd drive myself too.

By the time we got to the water fountain, she'd managed to walk off most of the cramp. Then I went with her to the nurse's office, where Nanette got her knee bandaged. The bell had rung for the end of class, and the hallway was already flooded with kids.

Nanette staggered when someone bumped into her. I automatically put an arm around her to hold her up.

She shoved me away. "I don't want your help! Aunt Silana and Miss Drake are enemies, so that makes us enemies too."

"Not *the* Miss Drake," a voice drawled. "Swing me around, will you, Ramirez?"

Mr. Ramirez was a short, balding man in his thirties who taught social studies. He was pushing an AV cart out of a classroom. Instead of a television and a DVD player, the cart carried the *Speculum Temporis*—though everyone called it the Magic Mirror. It was about a foot high and rectangular, with rounded corners and points in the middle of each of its four sides. Its gilt frame was decorated with never-ending spirals.

The mirror let you see through time. Ms. Kululu had already brought it into English class so we could ask Shakespeare some questions about *Romeo and Juliet*.

And when we had to do reports on the American colonies, I enjoyed chatting with Benjamin Franklin, whom I found rather clever, but practical too.

Mr. Ramirez turned the cart so we could see an elderly man in the shimmery surface of the mirror. His suit was as white as vanilla ice cream, and his hair and mustache almost matched it. When I heard the cicadas chirping, I knew it must be summer where he was. I hadn't heard them since we'd come to California.

"Mr. Twain," Mr. Ramirez said, and motioned his hand toward me. "This is Miss Drake's friend, Winifred Burton."

Mark Twain's mouth stretched into a broad grin. "And how is the old gal? Is she still tearing around the town upsetting apple carts?"

I scratched my head. "I've seen her tear up junk mail, but that's about it. Are we talking about the same Miss Drake?"

Mark Twain's eyes twinkled. "I'm talking about the Miss Drake who's one ton of bad temper with wings."

"That's her, all right." I nodded. "But how did you get to know her?"

"I met her back when I was a newspaper reporter in San Francisco," Twain explained. "She persuaded me to keep quiet about certain things in exchange for a favor."

So Mark Twain knew about the magicals and the Agreement too.

Mr. Twain took a cigar out from inside a coat pocket. "Bet she never told you about the time she had to pretend to be a gargoyle."

Mr. Ramirez gave a polite cough. "Excuse me, Mark. Even though you're talking to us through the mirror, you're still technically in school, so no smoking."

"Oops. Sorry, I keep forgetting." Mr. Twain tucked the cigar back inside his coat and then grinned at me. "Well, sir, she got lost in the fog one night and bumped her head. And when she came to in the morning, she was in the dirt at the site where a church was being built. Miss Drake was so covered in dust, the workers thought she was waiting to be hoisted up to the roof as a rain-spout. She had to lay there the whole day with her mouth open."

I folded my arms. "I think your nose is growing, Mr. Twain."

"Is it?" He rubbed his nose. "Well, they didn't call me the Human Sundial for nothing. On a sunny day, my family never looked at a clock. They just had me stand outside and then checked the shadow made by my nose."

"Of course, you must have known the Voisins too," Nanette said.

Mr. Twain smiled politely. "Can't say I do, but then San Francisco was a busy place, and people were coming and going all the time."

Nanette looked irritated. Being ignored was worse than being gossiped about.

Suddenly, the bell rang for next period. "Sorry to interrupt, Mr. Twain. Thanks so much for talking to my class, but I'm going to turn off the mirror and let you go now. I'm supposed to be giving a test to sixth graders."

As Mr. Ramirez started to reach toward the mirror to shut it off, Mr. Twain held up a hand. "Any chance I could chat some more with Winnie?" To Nanette's even greater annoyance, he added as an afterthought, "And Nanette too."

Nanette was used to being the center of attention so that didn't put her in the best mood. But she said, "Mr. Ramirez, my aunt, *the* Silana Voisin, has the same kind of mirror. I know how to turn it off when Mr. Twain wants to go. If you'll just tell our math teacher, Mr. Sebesta, that we'll be late."

"I'd be much obliged," Mr. Twain said.

"All right, Mr. Twain. Why don't you talk with Winnie and Nanette while they wheel you to the AV room?" He nodded to us. "I'll poke my head into Mr. Sebesta's class on my way to my own."

As we wheeled the cart through the now empty halls, Mr. Twain cleared his throat. "Hope you don't mind some friendly advice from someone who made the same mistake you're making. You can dislike one another without being enemies. Why not be adversaries instead?"

"There's a difference?" I asked.

"The difference between an adversary and an enemy is like the difference between a pebble in your shoe and a boulder on your back," Mr. Twain explained. "You can still get somewhere despite the pebble, but the boulder won't let you get anywhere. Just ask Mr. Sisyphus."

"Sissy-who?" Nanette asked.

In a book of Greek myths, I'd read about Sisyphus. "He was a prisoner who had to roll a boulder up a hill every day, but it always rolled back down again." Too late, I realized I had shown up Nanette again.

But all Nanette said was "Oh."

Mr. Twain nodded. "You can learn things even from an adversary, Miss Nanette. And an adversary can make you try harder and become even better."

So I held out my hand to Nanette. "So it's adversary city, then?"

Nanette hesitated until Mr. Twain warned, "Stay enemies, and you'll be so busy hating one another that you won't have time for anything else."

Maybe Nanette was thinking of her real goal: saving her mother. Nothing, not even me, was going to get in the way of that.

"Let's be frenemies," Nanette suggested, shaking my hand, "not enemies."

We thanked Mr. Twain for his advice, and he nodded. "Till next time, ladies."

When Nanette touched the point on the top of the frame, the surface shimmered, and we were looking at our own thoughtful reflections.

"Have you tried looking for your mom in that?" I asked.

Nanette shrugged. "Yes, but I didn't see anything."

The AV room had equipment that you could have found in any school, like portable speakers and other stuff. But it also had magical gear, like the carton of leathery eggs marked *Memory Eggs*—whatever they were.

I rolled the cart into an empty space by a wall, and Nanette said, "I just want to check if my dad is really going to ground me through the holidays like he says he will."

The metal frame was fancy with curving lines and points. Nanette's fingers touched different parts of it as she murmured an enchantment.

Her reflection shimmered and then disappeared as the surface clouded.

"I was going to spend the holidays with my cousins in France," she explained as she waited, "but my dad said after you-know-what happened, we wouldn't."

Her reflection disappeared in boiling clouds of colors and then sharpened into the picture of Nanette walking with a group of people through a set of gates with a sign reading PARC DISNEYLAND.

"Yay, Dad changed his mind. That's the Disneyland in France." Nanette seemed very pleased and excited as she pointed at some girls our age. "And those are my cousins." She folded her arms. "The mirror only shows you a possible future, so I'll have to be real careful what I do from now until December."

Suddenly I felt like a bunch of ants were racing under my skin. I hadn't realized the Magic Mirror could look forward as well as backward. "How far into the future can you see?"

"The farther you try to look, the more power you need and the more complicated the spell becomes." Nanette glanced at me sideways. "A month or two is all I can manage. If you're thinking about checking on Nessie's prophecy, that probably won't do you much good."

"I'd still like to try," I said.

Nanette didn't mind showing that she could do something I couldn't. "We have to give the mirror a specific amount of time, and we have to frame the question very carefully."

"Then please ask it what I'll be doing at Christmas," I suggested.

"Okay . . . for my frenemy," Nanette said.

I waited impatiently while Nanette worked the spell again, but this time there were two pictures in the mirror instead of one.

On the left, I stood near a tall Christmas tree in our living room, surrounded by my classmates. We seemed to be laughing and having a good time.

But on the right, I was in a tall building, alone and miserable. It made me think of a princess locked up in a tower. Through the window, I could see water and the Statue of Liberty. What was I doing in New York?

Nanette drew her eyebrows together in puzzlement. "Huh, I've never seen a magic mirror do that before. It looks like your future could go either way."

I pointed to the happy scene. "How can I make that one come true?"

"I don't know, but whatever it is, you've got to do it before Christmas," Nanette said as she turned off the mirror. "I'm sorry."

And this time I could tell that she really was.

* * *

Later that afternoon when I asked Miss Drake about what I saw in the mirror, she rested her muzzle on her paw. "Hmm, tell me the exact wording of your question."

When I told her, Miss Drake lifted her head confidently. "Ah, you see, that's where you went wrong. You left me out of the equation. The mirror showed you what might happen if you were left alone to your own devices. If you had asked it what you and *I* would be doing at Christmas, you would have seen just the happy future."

"Well, Nanette said I had to be careful how I framed my question," I said.

"Exactly. Other creatures may be victims of fate, but a dragon makes her own destiny." She set her claw tips against her forehead like a fortune-teller seeing my future. "And I am destined to celebrate Christmas here with you, your mother and your friends." She lowered her paw. "You have my promise."

I figured Miss Drake knew a lot more than any old mirror. And if you can't trust a dragon, whom can you trust?

So I did.

CHAPTER TWELVE

A smart pet will never fail to surprise you.

MISS DRAKE

As I sat, stuffed, at the Thanksgiving table, I had a lot to give thanks for. Right after Halloween, Pete and Abe packed up and left San Francisco. I thought we had beaten Jarvis. And Winnie and Liza were already looking ahead to Christmas.

"It's our favorite time of year," Liza

explained. "Do magicals celebrate Christmas, Miss Drake?"

I dabbed my napkin against my lips to wipe away the last crumb of pumpkin pie. "Some do and some don't."

"What about you, Miss Drake?" Liza asked pointedly. She was still trying to find out what I was. I'd already caught her making sure my human form had a reflection in the hall mirror.

"I celebrate Christmas just like you do," I said, plus many other holidays I had enjoyed during my travels. One can never have too many occasions to honor life— and enjoy a feast.

Liza set her fork down. "Winnie, you said the sky's the limit, so let's get a real tree that touches the ceiling." Since the ceiling in the living room was fifteen feet high, they were going to need a giant or at least a small crane to lift it.

Winnie stared at her half-eaten pie. "What's wrong with our regular one?"

"It's getting old, and the angel on top is kind of rag-gedy," Liza said. "I keep having to glue on her wings."

"But Daddy made it," said Winnie, stabbing her pie with her fork.

Liza sucked in her breath as if Winnie had just punched her. Then she laced her fingers together on top of the table. "Well, why don't we have two trees this year?"

I saw Winnie smile then, as if the idea of a big tree would be fine with her, as long as her dad's tree also had a place in their celebrations and hearts.

Vasilisa had brought in a fresh pot of tea. "Is there anything special Madame would like for her Christmas dinner?"

Liza thought a moment and then set both palms down on the table. "Yes, I'd like to have you and Paradise as our guests."

Vasilisa nearly dropped a swan-shaped creamer in her astonishment. "Who will make the food? Who will serve it?"

"You deserve a holiday too," Liza said. "We'll have it catered."

Vasilisa's eyebrows rose like war banners. "Strangers? In my kitchen?" She made it sound as if Liza were going to hire a cyclops to cook. Cyclops can be perfectly nice, but they aren't very fussy about what they choose for their meals or how they prepare them.

"It's just that we think of you like family," Liza said clumsily.

"Thank you," Vasilisa said. "Then, as family, you will understand when I say no."

"Maybe you could at least join us for dessert," Winnie suggested.

As Vasilisa cradled the bowl against her apron, I thought I saw her doll squirm inside the apron's pocket. "I accept."

Winnie leaned forward eagerly. "What would you like for Christmas, Mom? Remember, the sky's the limit." She was probably thinking of Clipper's Emporium floating in the clouds when she said that.

"Make me something, sweetheart," Liza said.

"You always say that," Winnie complained. "This year I can actually buy you a present."

"Something fun or pretty, then," Liza said. "And what would you like?"

"I've got to think about that," Winnie said. "Hey, let's go shopping downtown tomorrow."

"I wish I could," Liza said regretfully, "but I've already promised to help Rhiannon. She has a huge group coming in to ride."

I cleared my throat. "I could take Winnie window-shopping if you like."

Liza looked at me gratefully. "Would you?" Then she turned to Winnie. "We'll do something special another day."

"Okay, Mom," Winnie said.

As we flew over the downtown sidewalks the next morning, Winnie exclaimed, "Look at all the people. I've never seen such crowds."

It was Black Friday, the day after Thanksgiving, and all the bargain hunters were out early. Rivers of shoppers flowed from store to store. None of the shoppers looked up, but even if they had, we were hidden by my spell.

"The crowds are why we'll save downtown for another day," I said, and flew toward the bay.

"Where are we going?" Winnie asked. "Clipper's?"

"We'll go there soon," I said, "but the silkies' Aonach is once a year, and today is the day."

"What's an A . . . A . . . Ao—?" Winnie tried to ask.

"It's a fair that the silkies hold at Goat Island," I explained.

One question always led to another with Winnie. "And what are silkies?"

I pointed down to some lookouts lying on some rocks in the bay. "Those are silkies."

"They look like seals," Winnie said.

"When they wear their fur capes, they look like seals," I said. "But when they take them off, they look just as

197

human as you. But all the undersea folk come to buy and sell and trade. Merpeople, the naiads—everyone."

The water looked cold and uninviting, a dull gray-green like pea soup. It lapped at the piers of the Bay Bridge and around the hilly sides of Goat Island, which naturals also called Yerba Buena Island.

I eased into the bay, careful not to make a splash. There wasn't a ripple that might make a human on a passing ferry curious.

I floated for a moment, letting my body adjust to the coolness and enjoying the feeling of being in the ocean once again. The bay was always murky, but my dragon eyes easily adjusted to the dimness. In the distance, I thought I saw the silhouettes of a whale caravan carrying fairgoers and their goods.

I'd used a separate spell to make sure Winnie stayed warm and could breathe as we dived down, but I still craned my neck around to check. "Are you all right?"

Winnie's frizzy hair floated around her like seaweed, the brown strands looking like ribbons of dark ink. The colors of the land change when they enter the sea.

"I'm fine," Winnie said, bubbles of air rising like a string of crystal beads. "Whoa. The island didn't look like much. But down below, it's a regular mountain."

As cloudy as the water was, it was impossible to miss the mass of rock rising from the shadowy bay floor.

"That's because you just see the top of the island when we're flying. There's a lot more to it under the water," I said, and began to swim toward the Aonach.

A dozen seal-like silkies nearly collided with us as they arrowed toward the entrance in Goat Island. Hurriedly, I became visible again and just in time.

A merfamily swerved around us in the last moment, the mother and father nodding to us politely while the children whirled eagerly in circles.

Winnie started to get excited. "What are we waiting for?"

With a kick, I dived toward the entrance, passing a dolphin with a passenger upon her back.

"Morning, Miss Drake," Cullen said. "Welcome to your first Aonach, Winnie."

"Good morning," I answered. "Why aren't you in your nursery selling live trees in tubs?"

Cullen laughed a huge cloud of bubbles. "My workers will. I never miss the Aonach."

As soon as we swam through the entrance into a large vestibule, music and happy voices flooded around our ears. A soft, colored light came from the bioluminescent worms that grew above, their flowerlike mouths making the ceiling look like a garden turned upside down.

Some of the silkies were taking off their fur capes to reveal their human forms. I suppose they found hands and feet more useful for dancing and shopping.

The Aonach was held in the Silkie Cultural Center, which was carved into the stone. The biggest room in the cultural center was the dance hall. The silkies loved to dance, and since they could dance in three dimensions—up, down, and all around, as they said—the hall was almost as high as it was wide.

A small band of musicians was playing a sprightly reel on drums, gongs, bells, and conch shells, and the water of the hall was filled with twirling creatures. Peddlers and merchants had set up stalls in several rows one above the other along the walls.

"I want a real *zinger* for Mom's Christmas present," Winnie said.

I waved a paw at the stalls all around us. "You're surrounded by treasures from the Seven Seas. If you can't find *zing* here, I don't know where you'll find it."

But then Cullen sidetracked us by holding out a hand to Winnie. "My lady, will you dance with me?"

Cullen took both of Winnie's hands in his and guided her up in a wide, gentle loop.

"It's almost like flying," said Winnie, grinning. "Join

us, Miss Drake." And with a whip of my tail, I slid over next to them, undulating alongside as they circled and spun through the water.

Winnie was panting by the time the reel ended and seemed glad to turn Cullen over to the dozen silkies and merwomen and nereids waiting for a turn with him.

After a brief rest, we went shopping. I would have gone methodically along the rings of stalls along the walls, beginning with the lowest circle and working our way to the top. But Winnie was like a magpie, darting now here and now there as things caught her fancy—precious lumps of ambergris spat up by whales, pet sea hares that capered about in gaudy fringed skins that looked like tiny clown costumes, and even diamonds as big as my paw that brave fire salamanders had fetched from the molten insides of the earth.

"Ah, Miss Drake, I haven't seen you in a long time," a man called.

I turned to see Nanaue the shape-shifting shark waving me over to his stall.

To avoid scaring away customers, Nanaue had taken human form, but even without his pale gray skin, I would have known him by his double rows of pointy teeth. Unlike other sharks, his prey was your wallet rather than you.

Nanaue's nostrils widened as he sniffed at us—and

our money. "Come! Come! I've got everything you need for holiday presents."

Nanaue's was the last place I would shop. He got his wares cheap from student sorcerers, and it showed. There were stone garden gnomes that made rude noises. A wand swayed back and forth by itself as if conducting an unseen tinny orchestra, playing "Some Enchanted Evening." In honor of San Francisco, small wooden cable cars zoomed about like unguided missiles.

Nanaue dodged one of the cable cars to snatch the wand from the air and hold it out to me. "Now this is quality magic. It can play five tunes."

"And all of them equally off-key, no doubt," I sniffed. "Come, Winnie."

But Winnie had drifted over to a wooden box on the counter that was full of black chunks of volcanic rock, bearing a sign: THE LAST AND GREATEST MARVELS OF THE MASTER OF LAKI.

The Master had been a famous sorcerer and silversmith who had made a pact with fire elementals so he could create his magical masterpieces in the heart of an Icelandic volcano. But one day, his forge exploded, and he disappeared.

With a kick of his legs and a twist of his torso, Nanaue slid over to the box. "Your little friend has a good eye,

Miss Drake. Behold! All that remains of the Master's forge. Who knows what wonder each piece contains? And once they are gone, there will be no more."

I laughed skeptically. "Are they really from Iceland? Or did you swipe them from someone's rock garden?"

Glad to capture our attention, Nanaue spun happily. "Hoo, hoo, hoo. You are very funny."

I tried to nudge Winnie along, but she grabbed the edge of the table, holding on tight as a limpet at low tide. "Was it hard to get the rocks?"

Nanaue nodded cheerfully. "Yes, yes, very hard. The surface of the volcano was very hot and very sharp."

"Oh no." Winnie sounded distressed. "Did the volcano cut your feet?"

Nanaue tapped his forehead. "I was too smart for that. I wore wooden clogs, but it was hard to run in them when the Fire Giant chased me." He spun an elaborate tale of his escape. "By the time I dived into the safety of the ocean, the soles of my clogs had almost burned away."

I was surprised Winnie didn't see through Nanaue's lies. "Gee, Mr. Nanaue," she said. "It's been a real treat to meet you. I'd like to get one of these to remember you by."

Nanaue's double grin widened as he darted in for the kill. "For you, a special price."

Before Nanaue tricked Winnie out of all her money, I demanded, "How much?"

"One hundred dollars," he said. "Just a minnow of a profit for me."

I was about to scold Nanaue for trying to cheat a hatchling, when Winnie heaved a big sigh. "Too bad. I don't have much money."

That was when I knew Winnie was up to something. Liza gave Winnie a generous allowance, but she hardly spent any of it. Years of tight budgets had taught Winnie to be thrifty. Though she could afford any checker set, she used the one her father had made her.

Nanaue drummed his fingers thoughtfully on the countertop and then shrugged. "As a gesture of friendship to you and Miss Drake, I will take fifty dollars. I have thirty baby sharks at home. They'll starve if I sell for less than that."

"Oh no, I couldn't do that to your family." Winnie began to glide away. "You'd better sell those rocks to customers who can pay you what you need."

Nanaue waved both hands for her to return. "Eh, it will do my sharklings good to eat seaweed this month. Forty dollars."

I watched in fascination as Winnie steadily beat the price down with a mixture of sweetness, sympathy, and firmness. Of course, Nanaue would make a profit no matter how little he got for the worthless rock.

Finally, Nanaue offered to sell her a rock for a single dollar.

"Thanks so much, Mr. Nanaue," Winnie said, and pulled two quarters from her pocket, "but all I can afford is fifty cents."

"Sold!" Nanaue's hand was a blur as he snatched the coins from Winnie's palm. Then he picked up the rock nearest him in the box. "Here. This will make an interesting souvenir."

"Yes, it's very interesting," Winnie said, "but I kinda like this little one." It was about the size of a baseball. Though time had worn off the rock's sharpest edges, she still handled it cautiously.

As we swam to a higher level of stalls, I shook my head. "What is fun, pretty, or zingy about a rock?"

"I saw something sparkle." Winnie began to examine it carefully. "But even if I'm wrong, you have to admit his story was worth fifty cents. And I kinda felt sorry for him."

"Sorry for a lying, cheating shark who'd sell his own mother for a dollar?" I asked in amazement.

"Mom and I went to flea markets all the time looking for bargains," Winnie explained. "Mom usually got stuff cheap, because before she began bargaining, she'd try to get to know the sellers. Nanaue's the kind of seller everybody avoids unless he has something that they want."

"He has only himself to blame."

"I know that speck's here somewhere. Yeah! See? Something's sparkling." Winnie pointed excitedly at a tiny silver fleck the size of a pinhead.

"That's just—" I began, when Winnie brushed a fingertip across the fleck.

It was as if she had unlocked a secret latch. Instantly, the rock crumbled into a cloud of dark dust that dissipated quickly in the water, leaving a silver egglike object in her palm.

"Amazing," I finished my sentence.

"But what is it?" Winnie brushed the dirt off, and with a click, the compact object uncoiled. Ribbons of tiny half-inch stars streamed outward, whirling in an intricate dance until they locked together into the hollow, foot-high shape of . . . Nessie.

"I was just wishing she was at the Aonach with us," Winnie said.

I shook my head in wonder. "This must have come from the Master's forge. He was famous for making Serpent Silver, which takes the form of whatever you're thinking. Well done, Winnie. Your fifty-cent investment is priceless."

"It's something both fun and pretty," she said, smiling. Stretching out her hand, Winnie tickled Nessie's side. Instantly the stars unraveled and took the form of an angel.

Winnie clapped her hands together happily. "It's perfect for the top of Dad's tree! He made us a cool one, but Mom's right about the old angel. She's going to love this." She touched the angel again, and it changed into my lovely profile.

As Winnie made my image grow a mustache, I was going to protest. Suddenly I felt my phone begin to vibrate. It was a gift from Reynard and worked as well in water as it did on land, and the message was from him.

R: Trouble! Check yur emails.

When I opened his email, I saw that he had attached a photo. It was like a jigsaw puzzle with most of the pieces still missing. But as I stared at the ones that were there, I thought I saw the stage in the Spriggs auditorium—and what might be Winnie's frizzy brown hair.

D: Where did you get this?

I waited impatiently, until I got his reply.

R: I checked online tech forums after Halloween.
Guy bragged about a client who wanted him 2
recover movies on broken experimental camera
that looked like a pair of eyeglasses. He got this
image, but I didn't think anything about it. A week
later, he bragged he'd gotten 60% of video.
Next day whole forum disappeared. That's not
supposed 2 happen. So I looked at picture again.

Jarvis had the money to make the impossible possible, so I tapped in with my claws:

D: Do you think Jarvis has video?

R: Don't know, tracking Jarvis now. Just bought
plane ticket 2 SF for tomorrow. Reserved Grand
Emperor Suite @ Newcastle Hotel.

I felt like my spine had turned to ice. Ever since Jarvis and Fluffy had quarreled over the way he was treating Liza, he had avoided San Francisco, not even attending his sister's funeral. There was only one reason he'd come here now: He was sure he could get Winnie.

The idiot didn't realize he was endangering not only

us but himself as well, for the High Council would deal viciously with any threat to Spriggs.

D: Who else knows about the video?

R: Anyone on forum.

The High Council had employees who searched the Internet and news services for stories about strange events in case one of them involved the magical clans. The employees, in turn, had a network of paid informants around the world who would pass on tidbits. It was quite possible one of those informants was a member of the tech forum just like Reynard.

I tapped with a vengeance:

D: Keep your ears open and your eyes wide for anything else. We have to destroy that video.

R: May B more than 1 copy? Backup copies could B on tablets, phones, in Cloud, on flash drives, etc.

It was like fighting a many-headed monster—or combing the snakes on Medusa's head on what she called a "bad hair" day.

D: We have to try.

When Winnie saw my face, she pocketed her Serpent Silver. "What's wrong?"

I had given her as much time as I could to enjoy her school, but now there was no choice. "I'll explain when we're back at home." I didn't want anyone here eavesdropping.

When she was safe in my apartment again, I made her tea and set out a plate of the little rose-shaped cookies she liked so much, filled with honey and raspberry.

But Winnie had no appetite. "Okay, why did we have to leave so early?"

"Reynard just wrote me that your grandfather has a video of the Halloween Festival at your school," I explained. "I suspect that a parent or student smuggled in an illegal camera. The camera looks like a pair of eyeglasses so it would be hard to detect." It was possible it was Mr. Cellini's new eyeglasses. "The video was damaged, and I don't know how much Jarvis has been able to reconstruct. But he's checking in to the Newcastle Hotel. I think he's ready to make a move."

She drew her knees up against herself and wrapped

her arms around her legs as if she was trying to become the smallest target. "Why?"

I couldn't sugarcoat the truth. "I think he plans to release the video about the strange things that go on at the school. He may even try to make people believe Spriggs is teaching you some kind of evil magic. Once he's darkened Spriggs's reputation in everybody's minds, he'll go to court to show why your mother is unfit because she sent you there."

Winnie protested. "Why is he doing all this? I don't think he even likes me."

I put my foreleg around her shoulders and gave her a hug. "He was always selfish, even as a little boy. What's his is his. His yacht. His Rolls-Royce. His granddaughter."

"But isn't Granddad scared of you?" Winnie asked.

"He only knows me in my human form as just another of his father's friends," I explained. "The only ones who saw my true form were your great-grandfather Caleb and Amelia." I added, "And now you."

Winnie chewed her lip. "How do we stop him, then?"

I sighed. "I wish your great-aunt Amelia had told me the secret word."

Winnie uncurled from the sofa. "What secret word?"

"I don't know," I said, "but it worked like magic. She'd whisper it in his ear, and he'd behave."

"We have to find out what that secret word is," Winnie said.

I shook my head. "That's gone with Amelia."

"Maybe we could ask her through a magic mirror like at school," Winnie suggested.

I shook my head. "I tried to speak to her once and all I got was a past adventure. The mirror only lets you talk to a few people it selects."

Winnie put her hands to her face in horror as a new thought occurred to her. "He could ruin everyone, Spriggs, my friends. And it'll be because of me."

"The High Council will never let it get that far," I said.

"They'll make him forget?" Winnie asked hopefully.

"And everyone else involved," I said.

"You mean, us?" she squeaked.

"Yes," I said, and then tried to reassure her, "You won't have to leave the mansion, and the High Council will arrange a transfer to a human school. You just won't remember me."

She wrapped her arms around me. "I don't want to forget you."

"And I don't want to forget *you*." I felt pearl tears beginning to sting the corners of my eyes, but this was no time to cry pesky gems. "So we'll nip this in the bud. Reynard and I will find every copy of the video and destroy them. Without it, Jarvis will sound like a crackpot, so he'll have to keep quiet on his own. . . ."

Winnie burst into tears. "But he could have hidden lots of copies of the video. Can you find them all in time?"

"I will do whatever it takes to stay with you," I promised, even if it meant biting or torching a few creatures along the way.

CHAPTER THIRTEEN

⁓ꙮ⁓

A pet that sticks to the chase is the one who wins the hunt.

⁓ Winnie ⁓

Miss Drake didn't have an appetite either, so she changed into her human form and we went upstairs. Both Paradise and Vasilisa were ready to do battle with Jarvis when Miss Drake told them the news.

"If that old turnip comes near, I'll dump a bag of manure on him, I will," Paradise swore.

"And I will show him a rolling pin can do more than flatten dough," Vasilisa vowed.

I was glad to hear they were on my side, but I couldn't wait any longer to ask them, "Miss Drake said that Great-Aunt Amelia had a secret word that would make my grandfather behave? Do either of you know it?"

Paradise shook her head. "No, Miss Winnie, but I wish I did."

"And I only came here after Mr. Jarvis had left," Vasilisa said, and then looked thoughtful. "But my mother worked here before me and so did Small Doll."

When Vasilisa took Small Doll from her apron pocket and set her on the table, I began to ask, "Small Doll—"

Vasilisa put up a hand. "No, we must make our request properly." So I waited impatiently as Vasilisa made some hot chocolate and served it in the special little cup, then set out a slice of cake on the best china. Only then did she dip her head and ask, "Small Doll, Small Doll, you must be hungry. Small Doll, Small Doll, you must be thirsty. Do you know the word that will make Mr. Jarvis stop?"

I waited breathlessly for the hot chocolate and cake to disappear, but no light appeared in Small Doll's eyes. The cup and plate remained unchanged. One minute. Two. Then five.

Finally, Vasilisa sighed. "Small Doll cannot touch the gifts if *she* does not know the word. I am truly sorry, Little Madame."

I was sorry too, but I managed to remember my manners. "Thank you for trying," I said to Vasilisa, and then with my finger, I nudged the cup and cake a little closer to Small Doll. "And please eat and drink anyway."

But the chocolate and cake just stayed there.

Vasilisa spread her hands. "Small Doll is so sad *she* cannot eat and cannot drink."

That has to be very, very sad, then.

As Miss Drake and I sat down in the living room to wait for Mom, I asked her, "What will happen to Paradise and Vasilisa if . . . well, you know . . ."

"If the worst happens?" Miss Drake asked as she put her arm around me. "The High Council wouldn't touch them because this is none of their doing, and they can be trusted to keep silent about what little they know. And the High Council's own households would revolt if they tried to take our friends. Paradise's relatives tend the gardens of many magicals, and Vasilisa's family cooks and cleans in many magical homes. So our friends will still be here to look after you."

"Will I remember Small Doll?" I asked.

Miss Drake shook her head. "No, she'll just seem like a toy to you."

I held on to a new hope. "But you'll still be in the

basement, and I'll be up here. So even if I forget you and you forget me, we're bound to bump into one another. Right?" When Miss Drake didn't answer quickly, I tried to prompt her again. "Right?"

She made a little croaking sound as if she had something in her throat. "I may have to travel for a while."

I knew how cold and hard it could be wandering around. At least when I did, I'd had Mom. Miss Drake would have no one—no one to teach her to have fun, no one to make her laugh.

And she'd be homeless.

When I'd first met Miss Drake, I thought she'd have piles of gold and jewelry lying around. Well, she did have the trunk full of tiaras, but they were prizes from the Enchanters' Fair. And it's not like she made a fuss about them.

The more I'd gotten to know her, though, I'd come to realize that she really had all sorts of treasures that she loved—her comfortable sofa, her grand music box, my portrait of her, even that old rug of hers.

"You belong here with me," I protested.

Miss Drake shrugged. "I've wandered around the world many times before this. I can do it again, but why are we talking about such a gloomy future? Reynard and I will never let it happen."

I shut up then, but I kept picturing what would happen

if she and Reynard could not stop my granddad: she'd be alone, faraway, and it would all be my fault. Without me, Granddad would have left Mom alone, and Miss Drake could go on living like she always had.

As I sat on the sofa, I tried to think of how I could help.

Of course—Great-Aunt Amelia's journal!

I had skimmed it all, mainly reading anything about dragons. I could have missed the secret word.

Impatient to begin searching, I began to thump my heels against the sofa with each tick of the clock on the mantel—until Miss Drake put her hand on my knee. "Stop that."

It didn't help any that Mom was an hour late getting home.

As soon as I heard the front door open, I called out, "We're in the living room, Mom."

"Traffic was murder," Mom complained. "I think the whole Bay Area was out doing their holiday shopping." When she stepped into the living room, she smiled at Miss Drake. "Oh, Miss Drake. I'm glad you stayed. How was shopping? Can you have dinner with us?"

"Thank you, but I have to go as soon as I explain a few things to you," Miss Drake said. "I know it will be a lot to take in, but I'll do my best to answer all your questions."

Then she told Mom about Granddad and his plot and the threat.

Mom looked stunned, then frightened. "When I found out about the magicals at Spriggs, I was afraid something like this would happen."

"Mom, a lot of my friends are magicals," Winnie pointed out. "And they treated you nice at the Festival."

"But they're also so powerful." Mom massaged her forehead. "Can't our lawyer, Dylis, do anything?"

"She will see to it that you remain here in comfort," Miss Drake explained. "You just won't remember some things."

"If they steal one day of our memories," Mom said angrily, "that's theft on a big scale."

"I suppose it is," Miss Drake admitted. "But you and Winnie will stay safe at least."

But Miss Drake wouldn't. I remembered Nessie's foretelling. I needed to be Miss Drake's shield, but how? Maybe if I knew the secret word.

Then a new and horrible thought came to me. "Mom, where does Granddad live now?"

Mom sounded distracted because she was still worrying about the High Council. "What? Uh, he's in Manhattan."

"Can you see the Statue of Liberty from his place?" I asked.

"The last time we visited, he was on the Upper East Side, but he could have moved since then," Mom said. "Don't worry. You're never going to have to live with him."

Things seemed to be coming apart. "What if Granddad offers to keep quiet if I go with him? Would the High Council make that deal?"

"The High Council wouldn't bargain because that leaves them vulnerable to future extortion and blackmail," Miss Drake said, but she didn't sound so certain now.

Miss Drake left shortly after that, but I knew she'd return to her apartment by the hidden tunnel. Then she'd begin working to stop Granddad.

In the meantime, Mom and I nibbled at dinner. She was still stunned and angry, and I was in a hurry to begin my hunt. Finally, after a miserable half hour for both of us, I got to go up to my room. Mom seemed just as anxious to head to hers.

As I climbed the stairs, I repeated Nessie's words with each step I took. *Ye shall also be the shield against the arrow, the locked door against the wolf, the stout wall against the flood.*

I couldn't leave everything to Miss Drake like I usually did. I'd made up my mind, and I marched down the hallway to my room and got Great-Aunt Amelia's journal from the desk drawer. It was a thick book, covered in blue silk with a ripply pattern. When she'd used up the last page, Great-Aunt Amelia had written on separate sheets of paper, folded them and stuffed them in the back. The spine had cracked, and there was a pink ribbon around the book to hold all the pages and papers together.

I untied the ribbon and carefully opened the journal. A warning was written in big block letters on the very first page.

AMELIA'S JOURNAL.
KEEP OUT!
THIS MEENS YU, JARVIS.

I couldn't help feeling for my great-aunt. Granddad had been a pest even back then.

The very first sentence was simple: *May 8, 1940. I am six yesterday. Mi cake was gud.* It was written in block letters like the warning.

So my great-aunt had started keeping the journal the day after her sixth birthday.

The next few pages were also written in the same style. They told me that Great-Aunt Amelia had gone downtown with her mother, or that she got a B on a spelling test at her school—it wasn't Spriggs, though.

About five pages in, my great-aunt had written, *I met a dragon today. Her name is Miss Drake.*

I wished she'd written more, but what could you expect from a six-year-old? As the pages went on, the block letters changed to cursive, and there was more and more detail about her adventures with Miss Drake. She also transferred to Spriggs and loved it.

While there was plenty about my great-aunt and Miss Drake, there was nothing about Granddad besides that first warning to him. I was three-quarters of the way through when I heard a knock on the door.

"Time for bed, Winnie," Mom announced.

"Okay, Mom," I said, even though I didn't intend to go to sleep.

Mom had opened the door about a foot wide and was watching me. I put the journal on the desk and went to the doorway to kiss her good night. "Don't worry, Mom," I told her. "Granddad's a jerk, and jerks never win."

Mom hesitated before she said, "Of course not."

She touched the silver medal that hung around my neck, rubbing her fingers against the winged foot, and smiled. "You haven't worn that in a while." It was the special medal that my dad's grandfather, a firefighter, had won, and my good-luck charm. I had put it on tonight after supper, because wearing it made me feel close to Dad. Also, I knew we needed all the good luck we could get.

Mom waited until I was under the covers and then turned out the light.

I counted to a hundred after she had closed the door. Then I quietly got the journal and a small flashlight and got into bed again. I pulled the quilt over my head and snapped on the flashlight so I could keep looking for clues. But I reached the last page and hadn't found any. My great-aunt's handwriting had gotten shaky by then, and she was worried about Miss Drake: *What will my dragon do without me?*

But she'd found a good answer. She'd left Miss Drake to me. And I was going to take care of her as long as Great-Aunt Amelia had.

I snapped off the flashlight then and pulled off the quilt. I'd gotten hot and sweaty under it, so it was nice to sit a moment in the cool air. The moon had risen, and a rectangle of silver light stretched from the windowsill and into the room.

This room had been Great-Aunt Amelia's before. I wondered if she could have hidden the actual word someplace in here. But where did you put something as precious as the secret word?

You'd put it where you kept all your treasures, of course—the same spot where you hid your journal. So I took the flashlight and slipped inside the big walk-in closet lined with shelves and racks for coats and dresses. We had boxed all of Aunt Amelia's clothes, put some in the attic, and given the rest to her favorite charity store. The closet was pretty empty now, so it was easy to walk to the window seat at the far end—a secret spot for both my great-aunt and me.

Snapping on the flashlight, I swept it over the wooden floor until I saw the board with the crescent-shaped knothole. In her last letter to me, Great-Aunt Amelia had told me where I would find her journal.

Getting on my knees, I pried up the loose board and held up the flashlight, but I couldn't see anything in the hole. Leaning over, I began to search with my hand for something hidden underneath the other floorboards.

I got excited when I felt an object with hard edges. I pulled it out eagerly. It was a notebook with a blue silk cover—just like the other. But the spine of this one was perfect, and it opened stiffly, as if it were almost new.

On the inside cover was a note:

Happy 6th Birthday from Poppa.

So this had been a gift from my great-granddad, Caleb, who was the dad of Great-Aunt Amelia and Granddad Jarvis. The very first page had the same block letters as the writing in the other notebook:

AMELIA'S JOURNAL

But there was no warning to my granddad to keep out.

The very next page had been torn out, and the rest of the pages were blank. Had Granddad written something rude on the missing page and my great-aunt had gotten rid of it? Or had Granddad taken the lost page because it had the secret word on it?

Either way, I think my great-aunt hadn't felt the notebook was safe enough to keep her secrets in. But she didn't want to throw it away, because it had been a birthday gift from her father. So she'd kept it but not used it. Instead, she'd begun writing in an identical notebook—only from then on she kept it hidden where her brother would never find it.

I sat back on my heels. I was so sure the word would be in this book. It was frustrating to get this close and not find it. I put the floorboard back and took the original notebook back to my desk. To my surprise, Small Doll was sitting on top of it next to an old, dusty mouse's nest.

Her eyes flashed brighter than the beam of the flashlight.

Small Doll cleaned up messes, not made them, so the nest must have been pretty important. It was made out of tiny twigs, dried grass, string, and other odds and ends. But I also saw little bits of paper woven within it too.

When I teased one out, I saw it was a scrap of torn paper. On it was an *H* in block letters just like the early writing in the journal.

"This is amazing," I said with new hope. "Where did you get this from, Small Doll?"

The next moment, she had disappeared from the desk, and I heard a soft tapping sound. When I looked in that direction, I saw her standing by the wooden board at the base of the wall.

"Did this nest come from inside the walls?" I asked.

The eyes flashed what I guessed was a yes.

"How did you know it was there? Did you search inside the walls?" I wondered.

Again the eyes flashed.

"Thank you, thank you," I said. I was going to pick her up, but she had vanished. "Small Doll?" I asked, shining the flashlight all around.

But she was gone. Well, she had a house to keep clean too.

I rummaged in a desk drawer for a pair of tweezers that I remembered seeing. Then I pulled the nest apart, looking for little bits of white paper. Some of them were so small that I could have fit four on my fingertip. Whoever had torn apart the paper had wanted to destroy it. But I guess a mouse had found the pieces and taken them behind the wall to use in her nest.

Once I had every scrap I could find, I'd start to put them together like a jigsaw puzzle.

I was good at puzzles. My dad had always been able to get them cheap at the thrift stores, and we'd have a lot of fun evenings doing the puzzles. Sometimes, when pieces were missing or two puzzles had gotten mixed together, it had been a real challenge. But we'd always managed.

I fingered my medal and hoped I'd be lucky. Maybe, just maybe I could find out the secret word that would make Granddad go away.

∽ MISS DRAKE ∾

As I left the house, I felt sorry for Liza. She'd had to adjust to a lot of things in such a short time. If I'd had my way, I would rather she had never found out about the threat of the High Council, but I knew she wouldn't panic. She was too strong a woman for that, and her strength came from her determination to protect her daughter.

As I neared the grove of trees that hid the tunnel entrance, the last thing I expected was to see Reynard sitting on a park bench with his luxuriant red tail draped over the back and one hind leg crossed over the other. While I had taken human form, he hadn't bothered to change his shape.

I frowned. "Shouldn't you be in disguise?"

"Chillax. City people can't tell the difference between a fox and a dog as long as I've got this." He jingled the little metal license tag attached to a red leather collar around his neck. "Woof, woof." Then he held up a jar. "I thought you might want to help me bug the Jarvis's suite. He won't arrive for another hour."

I stared at the dozen cockroaches crawling around the bottom of the jar. "This is no time for pranks. Those are real bugs."

"Three to one that some security goon sweeps the rooms for listening devices when Jarvis stays there, so I hired these guys from a friend." Reynard grinned as if he had the answers—which he often did. "The goons'll never notice them listening to every word and watching."

"And how are they going to tell you what they found out?" I asked. I wouldn't put it past Reynard to equip them with tiny phones.

"Easy," he said. "The Newcastle keeps a beehive on the roof so guests can have real honey. I already made a deal with the queen."

"Well, don't try to bug my house. Small Doll will have your hide," I warned.

Reynard gave a little shudder. "I wouldn't think of it." He sprang off the bench onto his hind paws. "Well, are you going to give me a lift?"

"They'll never let a dog into the hospital," I said, and held up a hand as he started to object. "And no, I'm not going to pretend to be blind so you can be my guide dog."

I can change shape quickly, but I'm a sluggard compared to Reynard. He hopped over the back of the bench, and the next moment he called to me, "Pick me up."

When I went around the bench, I saw that he had turned himself into a large handbag that was a squat caricature of my real self. Two little hind paws extended out from the bottom, and two little forepaws thrust out from the scaly leather side. The clasp on top was a caricature of my elegant head.

"You're not half as funny as you think you are," I said, picking him up.

Carrying him, I walked over to the hospital and took the elevator to the roof where I set him down. Careful to keep my back to him, I made the signs of the spells and mouthed the words that changed myself into a dragon.

In the old folktales, foxes stole food or even gold, but Reynard was one of the modern breed who stole information.

When I turned around, he had changed himself into a fox with aviator's goggles and was fluffing out his tail.

Then we flew over the city's hills and small valleys. I remember when great sections had just been weeds and the occasional shrub struggling up out of the sandy soil. Now three- and four-story buildings clustered everywhere. Even in the little neighborhoods, the sidewalks were packed with shoppers, some doing their food shopping but many buying gifts from the small stores.

Ahead of us the Newcastle Hotel spread its bulk across an entire block like a fat hen settled on her nest.

Landing on the roof, I changed myself into an elegant lady in her fifties while Reynard picked the lock on the door leading to a stairway. Then he got on all fours as he pretended to be a dog again. "You have more shapes than I have," I grumbled to him. "Quit being lazy."

"Hey, this is a new disguise," Reynard shot back. He jingled the new medal he had added to his collar. "See? Best in the dog show. I'm a pure pedigree whatever."

"That medal still won't save a scruffy animal like you from the dogcatcher," I said.

Once inside the hotel, it was a simple thing to hop into an elevator.

Again, Reynard had no trouble picking the door lock to the Grand Emperor Suite. It consisted of a large, tastefully furnished living room with three bedrooms, two bathrooms, and a kitchen.

Just as Reynard had finished planting his bugs, we heard the door click as someone unlocked it. "Into a bedroom," I insisted, getting the empty jar.

We left the bedroom door open a crack to peek out and saw a maid roll a cart toward the kitchen. "I don't see why the guest has to have the fridge stocked before he gets here."

Another maid followed her with a second cart. "For what he's paying, he can have an elephant in the bathtub. Now scoot."

When they had disappeared into the kitchen, Reynard

nudged me. "Hey, I bet I can change into a maid faster than you can."

"We don't have time for games." Grabbing him by a foreleg, I picked him up and flung him around the back of my neck so his tail hung down one shoulder and his head and forepaws down the other. "Stop squirming and lie flat."

He went limp but said, "Fur's out of fashion on the West Coast."

"Then pretend I just flew in from Boston," I said, and hurried from the suite.

Walking down the hallway, I found the elevator and pushed the button. As we waited, Reynard began scratching his nose.

"Stay in character," I snapped.

"But it itches," he complained, and kept scratching.

He was still scratching when the elevator doors opened. Inside was a blond woman of about thirty in a white dress. Her eyes widened. "Your fox stole is still alive," she gasped.

I tapped Reynard on the head, and he let his paw go limp. "Thank you. I had no idea."

"I . . . I think I'll wait for the next elevator," she said as she stepped out of the elevator and into the hallway.

"Suit yourself," I said, and got into the elevator. When the doors closed again, I demanded, "Reynard, are you going to stay still or do I really have to knock you on the head?"

He didn't answer, and he didn't move again. Good.

CHAPTER FOURTEEN

*No two pets are alike. Each one will delight you
and get into mischief in quite a unique way . . .
you can count on it.*

⁓ Winnie ⁓

The house was real quiet, like it
was holding its breath while
each of us got busy work-
ing on ways to stop
Granddad Jarvis.

Mom and Miss
Drake seemed to
be keeping me out
of the loop for the
moment, so I didn't

tell them what I was doing. Anyway, I couldn't be sure if the scraps of paper contained the secret word or not.

I stayed up in my room and worked on my paper puzzle. Vasilisa brought my meals up on a tray, and I made sure to leave a little bit of everything for Small Doll, who popped up now and then to keep me company.

I began with the border, of course, and then tried to fit pieces to the scraps along the edge. Regular jigsaw pieces snapped into place, but it was hard to make sure these edges matched. I did a lot of leaning over and squinting. By the time I was halfway done, I realized my neck and head ached.

I decided to get up and stretch, but I did it too fast and created a breeze that blew the paper every which way. I'd have to start over. I almost cried. But this wasn't time to be a baby. If I wanted to be *the shield, the door, the wall,* I couldn't give up trying to find the secret word.

I hunted around through the desk drawers until I found a magnifying glass and some clear pockets Great-Aunt Amelia had put photos in.

I took an empty pocket and put it over the pieces on the desk. Perfect! They'd stay in place now whenever I got up to stretch or take a break.

Gently, I lifted the pocket, sat down, and got to work.

....

⟿ MISS DRAKE ⟾

That Saturday was busy. First, I went with Liza and Dylis to meet with Ms. Griffin at Spriggs. All things considered, Ms. Griffin took it very well. "Problems like this have happened before—though perhaps not as high-tech. Spriggs has always managed to weather the storm."

I cleared my throat. "We'll try our best to handle this without alerting the High Council."

"I understand," Ms. Griffin said, "and thank you for warning me."

Afterward, Liza went with Dylis to her offices to talk over legal strategies while I went back home. I'm afraid I didn't have time for Winnie even though this was all about her. I was too busy calling in favors from friends who I knew would keep quiet about this, or texting Reynard. So far all he had found out was what food Jarvis had ordered from room service and future plans for the board meeting of his company, Magjar.

I thought I should warn Silana that that there was a picture of her niece performing magic at the Halloween Festival and that there was also part of a video. So I sent her a text with the picture attached. But I didn't want her quick-on-the draw wand hunting down Jarvis. So I finished the message by writing:

> **D:** I'll handle. Copies might be placed with 3rd parties. If anything happens to owner of the video, 3rd parties will release video.

However events unfolded, I was pretty sure the High Council wouldn't punish Nanette. She'd been performing magic in an officially approved event even if the tricks themselves were unapproved. The one who was at fault was whoever had taken the video. And Jarvis, of course.

I had just sent it off when Reynard texted me.

> **R:** Remember geek from forum? He is pal of my friend. The geek's hopping mad, so he was glad 2 spill. His client wants total control of video, so there's only 1 version & it's on flash drive. Client's men broke down geek's door & checked all his equipment 4 copies.

One version? Jarvis trusted no one but himself, and he had made a bad mistake. Now we just had to find the eyeglass camera and the movie. And I'd bet anything that they were with him at the hotel.

....

᨞ Winnie ᨞

It wasn't until Sunday afternoon when the whole page took shape. There were still missing pieces, though, and a six-year-old's spelling wasn't great. So I read and reread what my great-aunt Amelia had written:

> I NO MI BROTHER'S BIG SECRET. LAST
> NITE I GO TO THE BATHROOM. I WALK
> BACK THRU THE HALLWAY. BUT I HEAR
> HIM TALK TO SUM1. I PEEKED THRU THE
> KEYHOLE.
> JARVIS STILL HAS A TEDDY BEAR. HIS
> NAME IS MAGNUS. H(E) LIKES 2 HUG AND
> KISS . . . TO BED WITH HIM.

There was a section missing after *kiss,* but I could guess my granddad took his teddy bear to bed with him.

If my great-aunt was six, my granddad would have been about twelve. I didn't see anything wrong with hugging and kissing a teddy bear at any age. But I thought about some of the boys at the schools I'd been at. They all wanted to look rough and tough, so they wouldn't be caught dead with a teddy bear. If they'd found out that one of them was sleeping with his teddy bear, they could have made his life miserable. (I bet a lot of those boys still had a stuffed animal they loved in private. But when they were with other boys, they pretended they didn't.)

Things probably were even worse years ago for a boy with a bear. I almost felt sorry for Granddad, because he had to hide his teddy bear.

What if the magic word was the name of Granddad's teddy bear? When Great-Aunt Amelia wanted him to behave, she simply said *Magnus* and that reminded Granddad that she knew his secret. No wonder Granddad had done whatever she wanted.

Granddad had sent Mom a letter right after Dad had died. She hadn't let me read it, but it had made her cry. I remember the envelope that the letter had come in. It was on his business stationery with a big black *M* with little triangles around the sides. I thought they'd been like the fringe around a curtain. Now I realized they might have been fangs.

I closed my eyes as I tried to picture the name next to the logo. Had it been the Magjar Corporation?

I did a search on my tablet. There was an article from the *New York Times* business section. It mentioned Granddad as the president of the corporation. I just had to laugh.

He'd named this huge company after his teddy bear.

But then I read on. His company seemed to do a lot of things, from making fighter jets to junk food. But all the different divisions had one thing in common. The article quoted various experts who used words like *ruthless, vicious,* and *without conscience* to describe the Magjar Corporation. *The mysteriously named Magjar,* one financial analyst said, *strikes terror in the hearts of companies everywhere.*

So Magjar was supposed to be ruthless, vicious, and without a conscience, but no one knew what the name meant. Except for me. *Magjar.* Granddad had combined his name with Magnus like they were a team.

Only I didn't think any self-respecting teddy bear would do stuff like that. It sounded more like the man who'd chased Mom and me across the country. And now that same man was willing to destroy the Spriggs Academy and hurt my new friends.

But what if people knew Granddad had a teddy bear

as a partner? At the least, Granddad would be embarrassed. Some people might feel silly for being so scared of a teddy bear's company.

At first, I was going to tell Mom and Miss Drake everything. Mom was a hard bargainer, but she had a conscience. She might not want to blackmail her father.

Blackmail wouldn't bother Miss Drake, of course. My dragon played by her own rules, not human ones. But Sir Isaac had spent a week teaching us that *for every action there is an equal and opposite reaction*. It is a fancy way of saying *push me and I'll push you*.

Miss Drake could hold off Granddad for a while. But from what I'd read, Granddad was a poor sport about losing. So I bet he'd start trying to get even by finding dirt on her.

If Granddad discovered Miss Drake was a dragon, he could threaten to reveal her secret. I could picture hordes of reporters and cameras surrounding our home. Poor Miss Drake would hate that, and before long, someone would get nipped or roasted to a crisp.

And I couldn't see the High Council letting that go on for long. There'd be a massive loss of memories, and Miss Drake would be sent wandering. I almost cried at that thought.

But that left only me to face Granddad. The idea made me shiver.

Strange, isn't it? I went to school with students that other humans might have called monsters, but they were just my schoolmates. The real monster was a human who was my own grandfather.

But what if I met with Granddad, and I was wrong about the secret word? Would he drag me back to that lonely tower in New York?

Wouldn't I be safer staying here and leaving everything to Mom and Miss Drake after all? Nessie's prediction popped into my mind then. I wasn't supposed to be a turtle hiding in my shell. She had actually been warning that it would be up to me to defend everyone I loved, especially Miss Drake.

And when you love someone—really love someone—you'll do anything to protect them. I had to stop thinking about what was best for me and start thinking about what was best for my dragon. As awful and lonely as that New York future looked, I'd put up with it so long as Miss Drake could keep on being Miss Drake. But it hurt to think it might be without me.

I checked where the Newcastle was and how to get there. All I had to do was catch the 1-California bus.

Then, to be on the safe side, I took a picture of the journal page with my phone before I hid the pieces in my great-aunt's secret spot. Finally, I picked up my wallet with my bus pass.

My great-aunt had left her dragon to me to protect, and now she'd indirectly left me the way to do that.

It was my job to stop Granddad. *Shield. Door. Wall. That was me.*

....

∾ MISS DRAKE ∾

B ased on my memories of our earlier jaunt, I had drawn the penthouse layout on my tablet. Reynard's bugs could tell us how many people were in the penthouse and where.

I was just setting my tablet down when Reynard texted me.

R: Jarvis has a box. No one else handles it.

D: What's inside?

R: Box is very tight. Not even my bugs can get in there.

That had to be very tight indeed because cockroaches can slip through the most miniature cracks.

243

D: That box has to have the camera and the flash drive.

R: When do we go?

I was going to write that we would do it tonight when I got a call from Liza.

D: Wait. Liza's trying 2 reach me.

When I answered Liza's call, she said frantically, "Winnie's gone!"

I swore to myself. Despite my warning, Winnie must have become restless and left the house. Now, when I should be setting up the raid, I'd have to hunt for her. "Did she say where?"

"Her note says she's gone to the Newcastle," Liza answered. "She's going to make her granddad stop from telling everyone about Spriggs. I'm afraid once she's with him, he'll take her away."

I clenched my paws, my claws digging into them. I was afraid of the same thing. "I'll go get her." I might be able to grab the video too, but freeing Winnie was the main goal now.

"I'll meet you there," Liza stated determinedly. "You'll need help."

I would at that. Someone had to get Winnie while I fought off Jarvis's thugs. There was no time to get Reynard. I didn't have a moment to lose. "We'll go together. Where are you?"

"In Winnie's room, but every second counts. I should leave for the Newcastle in my car now," she said. "The streets are going to be jammed with shoppers."

"I know a faster way," I told her. "I'll be with you in a moment."

Few naturals are as intelligent as Winnie and can see how beautiful we dragons are. I knew from personal experience that most naturals will scream their silly heads off when they see my true form.

I wanted to cushion the shock a little for Liza, so, as I raced out of my apartment and into the basement, I transformed myself into the human shape Liza knew.

Liza was just leaving Winnie's room as I came up the stairs to the second floor.

She stared at me, bewildered. "How did you get here so fast? And how did you get inside the house?"

"I live here too," I said. "Do you remember those stories that Amelia used to put into her letters to Winnie?"

Liza nodded. "Sure. She wrote about dragons, but they're just . . . make . . . believe." Her voice trailed off as the truth began to dawn on her.

"As make-believe as djinns and other magical

creatures. Just keep in mind that I love Winnie and would never let anyone harm her." I wished I could have taken longer to prepare her for the final secret, but I had no choice. I moved my hands and murmured the words. The world shimmered in a gold cloud, and there I stood in my full glory. "Dragons are as real as you are."

I tensed, waiting for Liza to holler or faint or both. But though her face had gone pale with shock, she took a stiff step toward me as if she was forcing her frightened legs to move. Then another and another as she worked up her resolve.

"You're not afraid of me?" I asked cautiously.

Liza swallowed. "Of course I am. You're a dragon." She pointed at my talons. "But you're on my side."

I should have realized how tough-minded she could be when it came to protecting her daughter. She went up another notch in my estimation. "Well done."

Liza fished her keys from the pocket of her jeans. "But I don't think you'll fit in my car."

"No need," I said. "I'll fly you there."

Her eyes went wide as saucers. "Me, fly on a real dragon?"

Her thrilled amazement reminded me of Winnie. Well, the apple doesn't fall far from the tree.

"Has . . . has Dad ever met you?" Liza asked.

"Many years ago as just another of his father's friends."
I waved a paw for her to follow me down the stairs. "And
never in my true form."

I didn't have time for my usual takeoff from the hospital roof so I'd have to take the risk. I'd make us invisible
before we went out into the backyard and launch us from
there. Once at the hotel, I'd make Jarvis sorry he had
ever tried to take Winnie from us.

CHAPTER FIFTEEN

❧

You can catch more flies with honey than with vinegar.

ADAPTED FROM *POOR RICHARD'S ALMANACK* BY BENJAMIN FRANKLIN

❧ Winnie ❧

I'd never been in a place as fancy as the Newcastle. It almost made me wish I'd changed into my best clothes before I came here.

But I told myself that as expensive as the lobby looked, none of the furniture was as wonderful as the treasures at Clipper's Emporium. You never knew if a carpet there was haunted by a ghost or a chair would fly around the room. After traveling with Miss Drake, it took more than fancy sofas to impress me.

When I found the front desk, I asked the clerk for Granddad's room number. The clerk was a thin man with a shaved head and so tall, he had a long way to look down his nose at me. "Young lady, we do not give out that kind of information."

But when you've ridden a dragon, had lunch with Nessie, and fought monsters, it would take more than a fussy hotel clerk to scare me away. I gave him my best imitation of Miss Drake's glare. "Jarvis Granger is my grandfather, and he'll be real mad if I don't get to see him."

I'd seen Miss Drake's glare make a giant take to his heels, bawling for his mommy. The clerk wasn't rattled by mine, but at least he asked, "Is he expecting you?"

I raised my eyebrows and glared harder. "No, but he'll want to see me."

Picking up a phone, the clerk called the penthouse. "Mr. Granger's granddaughter is in the lobby." When he hung up, his tone was respectful. "Someone will be right down to get you."

I went over to wait by a tall potted fern while I shaped my plan. It was comforting to feel my medal, a tiny shield of my own, heavy and warm below my throat. Dad would have hated what my grandfather was doing. *Wish me luck, Dad.*

"Ms. Burton?" a man asked a few minutes later, and I nodded. His muscular chest and arms looked ready to burst the seams in his suit coat. He must have had a bad case of dandruff, because his jacket was speckled with lots of little flakes.

"This way, please," Mr. Muscle said.

A smaller, younger version of Mr. Muscle stood by one of the elevators, blocking other people from getting in.

As I walked past the crowd and into the elevator, they scowled at me for hogging the elevator all to myself. When the Muscle Brothers joined me, Junior punched a button, and the doors closed immediately and we began to shoot upward.

When the elevator stopped, the doors opened, and I was led to a door with a brass plate that said THE GRAND EMPEROR SUITE.

The Muscle Brothers ran a card through the lock and swung the door open. "This way, miss."

They stepped aside and stayed out in the hallway as I entered, and the door shut behind me.

Granddad was sitting in a leather chair tall enough to be a throne. His body was thin and weak, so his head seemed bigger—like an upside-down scallion.

When I was a baby, my parents had taken me to meet

him, but I was too small to remember the visit. From what I heard, things got nasty, and my parents had never gone back.

My mother had no photos of him, but I'd seen a few of him as a boy in my great-aunt's family album. Grand-dad's face still had the same annoyed expression—like a fly had flown into his mouth.

On a small table on his left was a cube of some pol-ished reddish-brown wood that could have held a bowl-ing ball.

"Good afternoon, Winifred," he said. His voice creaked like an old leather harness that was about to crack and break. "Please sit down." He motioned to a sofa near him.

"Thank you." As I sat down, I stared at him.

At first, it was hard to believe he was the monster who had made life so miserable for Mom and me. But then his eyes blazed angrily. "I've wanted to see you for a long time. You've given me a lot of trouble and cost me a lot of money, young lady."

"Good," I said. "I wish we'd caused you even more trouble and cost you a lot more money."

When he frowned, all the lines around his mouth sagged like the skin of a prune. "I see your mother hasn't taught you about respect."

I quoted Miss Drake. "Respect has to be earned."

"Exactly," Granddad agreed. "And your mother threw away what little respect I had for her when she married that lazy artist."

It was my turn to frown and wrap my fingers tightly around my medal. "Dad painted beautiful pictures, and he wasn't lazy at all. He was always doing stuff with me when he wasn't painting."

"And died penniless," Granddad said. Money seemed more important to him than anything.

"He made us happy," I said, which was all that counted with me.

"Money *is* happiness," Granddad snapped. Nanaue would have agreed with him, which was fitting. The newspaper articles made Granddad sound like a shark among humans.

"No," I argued. "You can't be happy without friendship and love."

"It's what I was afraid of," he growled. "Your mother has filled your head with silly notions. But even a fool shouldn't have sent you to a school teaching evil magic."

On the bus ride here, I'd rehearsed what to say and do. "You're crazy."

He lifted his head triumphantly. "I saw what I saw. I have digital proof, a video in fact."

I followed the script of fibs I'd put together. "What

you saw was an act at the school festival. It's no more evil magic than an act in Las Vegas. All you saw was some stage tricks that the girl copied from her dad's act."

Granddad called my bluff. "You'll have to lie better than that, Winifred."

Well, the story had been worth a shot. Now it was all up to my great-aunt's magic word.

"Okay, I was trying to be nice, but you made me do this."

Granddad watched puzzled as I got to my feet and crossed the rug to his chair.

"Do what?" he asked nervously.

Leaning over, I whispered into his ear. "How's sweet Magnus?"

I waited tensely. Would his bear's name still threaten him? Or would he laugh?

Granddad reared back like I'd just tried to bite him. "How—?" he began.

Thank you, Great-Aunt Amelia!

I felt like I'd just triple-jumped across the checkerboard and gotten kinged. But I'd learned that when you're winning, you keep pushing—which is how I beat Miss Drake umpteen million times already. "I read all about you hugging and talking to him at night."

Granddad stared at me in amazement. "But I destroyed that page from Amelia's journal."

I corrected him. "You only thought you did."

"I made a deal with my sister," Granddad said angrily. "I would do what she wanted if she told no one. So she broke that promise, did she? What a brat she was."

"She kept her word." I took out my phone and showed him the picture I'd taken. "I found the pieces of the original page and put them back together."

He studied the image. "That's the page all right. Amazing. The last time I saw the pieces, they were in my trash can. How on earth did you get hold of them?"

I wasn't about to tell him about Small Doll. "One push of a button"—I held my finger up and gave it a twitch for emphasis—"and your secret is all over the Internet."

Granddad hunched his shoulders like I was going to hit him with a big stick. "You'll ruin me if you do. My enemies leave me alone, because they're scared of me. If they think I'm weak and sentimental, they'll team up to destroy me." He clasped and then unclasped his hands several times. "And what about all my people? I employ thousands. They'll be out of work if you send that story. You've got to delete it for their sake."

I knew Granddad didn't care about his employees. The articles I had read said many of them were suing him for the money he owed them. He wasn't worried about his employees any more than Nanaue had been worried about his babies. "You're the one who named the company and made the enemies, not me."

Granddad stopped pretending he was upset and sat up straighter. "Humph, you're not as soft as I thought."

"I won't tell anyone about Magnus if you won't show that video to anyone," I bargained. "Do we have a deal?"

Granddad's chin sank against his chest while he considered that. "Hmm, you're a pretty tough cookie. When I was your age, I would never have been clever or sneaky enough to uncover such a big secret like you did." He stared up at me. "In short, you're everything I want in a granddaughter . . . and yes, far more. You'll also be able to turn our enemies into toads."

I wanted to say that I couldn't do magic, but I saw the silver lining. "Does that mean you're going to leave Spriggs alone?"

"Of course," Granddad said. "Who's going to teach you useful curses?" He rubbed his jaw. "Hmm, I wonder if Amelia cast some spells on me?"

In her journal, my great-aunt had never mentioned enchanting anyone, so she hadn't had any more magic than me. But I didn't let myself get distracted. "You've got to destroy all the evidence."

"I need a little blackmail of my own just in case." The corners of Granddad's mouth curled up as if he were enjoying himself—like he was saying, *Every time you shove me, I'll shove back.*

I needed something else to make Granddad get rid of the stuff. I could threaten him since he thought I knew magic. He probably wouldn't like a set of boils in the shape of a Spriggs gargoyle.

But if I'd been nasty to Nanaue at the Aonach, would I have gotten the Serpent Silver? No, it would have made him raise his prices just to spite me. So bullying Granddad would just make things worse.

I had to act like I was at a flea market instead of on a battlefield. That meant following Mom's first rule of bargaining: think like the other person. What did Granddad need? What was he missing, and what could I do for him?

I doubted if someone as mean as Granddad had any friends. Most likely the only people around him were employees. They spent time with him because he paid them, not because they liked him. Everyone else would avoid him—just like everyone avoided Nanaue.

I thought of the lonely me I'd seen in the Magic Mirror. That had been a possible future for me, but for Granddad it was the real deal. Nobody should have to live like that.

"If you get rid of the evidence . . ." I hesitated a moment, wondering if I was going to be sorry about this later. "I'll . . . I'll write you." I was going to say, *I'll text,* but I doubted that he'd trust emails or texts.

That threw Granddad off balance because he had been expecting me to menace him rather than offer a trade. "What?"

I licked my lips nervously. "Since I'm staying here, and you're going to go back to New York, I thought you'd want to know how I'm doing."

Granddad looked as puzzled as a tourist trying to find his way around San Francisco with a Boston map. "I . . . uh . . . can get transcripts of your grades."

"Don't you want to know what I'm thinking and feeling too?"

He squirmed as if my question made him feel uncomfortable. "Whatever for?"

"What do you think would happen if I came to live with you?" I asked.

His hands tightened on the chair's arms. "I'd train you."

Maybe that's what had gone wrong between him and Mom. "You mean you'd give me orders and expect me to obey. But I'm not an employee; I'm your granddaughter. I've got plenty of thoughts and feelings, and you better believe that I'd make you listen to them. And," I added, "if I write you, you can write back."

"My letters would bore you," Granddad said defensively.

I felt like shaking him. "You need to talk to someone. You know, share things you see or feel."

His *humph* changed right in the middle to an *hmm*. "My letters will be private? You won't show them to anyone else?"

"They'll just be between the two of us," I promised.

He stared out the window, and I held my breath. Finally, he turned his head back to me. "We've got a deal."

Granddad twisted in his seat and reached for the box. As he undid the latch, I thought he had some super high-tech thingamabob in there. But when he swung the lid back, I saw the insides of the box were padded with purple silk. There was a cushion of the same material. On it sagged a little old teddy bear. He was missing fur in several spots, and his nose was threadbare.

His voice grew gentle. "Meet Magnus."

He must really have loved his stuffed animal. "You keep him with you?" I asked.

"Of course." Granddad set the bear on his lap. Magnus's black eyes caught the light, so they seemed bright and alive.

Maybe there *was* a little spark of life somewhere in Magnus too—the kind of spark that made people kind and thoughtful and trusting. Most people kept that spark inside them, but Granddad had locked his up in a box. It was like a fairy tale Dad used to tell me about an ogre who hid his heart in a jar.

Taking the cushion from the box, Granddad tore it open. In a flurry of feathers, he pulled out a flash drive and a broken pair of glasses in a plastic bag. "These are the only copies of the video."

As I took them, I asked, "You swear these are the only versions?"

Granddad looked hurt. "I promise I'm telling the truth. *You* have to trust me not to ruin you like *I* have to trust you not to ruin *me*."

I hesitated, but to seal this deal, a hug seemed better than a handshake. I put my arms around Granddad. His bony shoulders stiffened. "Sorry. You don't like hugs?"

He relaxed suddenly and patted me on the back. "I'm out of practice."

When I let him go, he put Magnus on what was left of the cushion, closed the lid, and locked the box. Poor little bear.

Suddenly there were thumps and grunts from the hallway, followed by silence.

"Pete," Granddad called, "what's going on?" When there was no answer, he tried the other Muscle brother. "Abe? Abe? Answer me."

"They can't," Britomart said as she walked into the suite and flung the key card on the floor. She was the big guard at Clipper's Emporium—except instead of her usual armor, she had squeezed all of her muscles into a stylish suit. I was pretty sure Britomart would never wear an outfit like that, so it must be Miss Drake. She'd flown here and then changed into her friend's shape.

Mom followed Miss Drake into the room. "Hello, Dad."

....

⤳ MISS DRAKE ⤳

"Liza?" Jarvis said in surprise. "What are you doing here?"

His voice creaked like a worn-out step on an old staircase, quite unlike the younger man I had known.

They say don't get between a mother bear and her cub, but at the moment, Liza was far more dangerous than any bear. "Winnie's leaving with me." As she stalked across the room, she seemed to get bigger and angrier. "So don't try to stop me."

I expected Jarvis to rage and throw a tantrum, but he merely raised a hand. "I wouldn't dream of it."

It was Liza's turn to be surprised. "What?"

Winnie was grinning from ear to ear. "Granddad and I made a deal."

Jarvis put his right hand on the wooden box solemnly. "Liza, I promise I won't make any more trouble for you or Winifred or her school. In exchange, Winifred has agreed to write me." He gave an embarrassed cough. "So I can check on her progress at school and such."

The box obviously held something that was important to Jarvis. But what? There were feathers on the floor below. But what was their significance?

"Winnie can stay with me?" Liza asked.

Jarvis smiled. "Despite all your efforts to ruin her, my blood has held true."

Liza stood uncertainly. "What do you mean?"

"She's tough, shrewd, and a bit ruthless." Jarvis waved his arm grandly. "She's the granddaughter I always wanted and everything I could wish for in an heir."

"What about the videos?" Liza demanded.

Winnie didn't look too happy at being called ruthless, but she held up the flash drive and the bag with the broken glasses. "Got 'em. Spriggs is safe."

I remembered Nessie's foretelling. I was the strongest in the room and Winnie the weakest, and yet she was the one who had beaten Jarvis. The "found will be lost" must be the video that Jarvis no longer had, but what was the "lost will be found"?

I sucked in my breath. *Had Winnie found the lost magic word?*

Jarvis winked at Winnie. "Winifred convinced me that the Academy is the perfect place for her education."

Liza took Winnie's hand. "How did you do it, Winnie?"

"That's between her and me," Jarvis said.

"Right," Winnie said with a nod. She sounded so firm about secrecy that I doubted any amount of arguing would get her to reveal what had happened.

As we exited the suite, I leaned over and murmured, "This is your best trick yet, Winnie. You made Jarvis disappear."

But then before the door completely closed, we heard Jarvis call, "Write me soon, Winifred."

"Well, almost." Liza sighed.

Pete and Abe were just starting to regain consciousness when the elevator came. As soon as the doors closed and we were riding safely downward, Liza frowned at Winnie. "That was a very foolish thing to do, Winnie.

Your grandfather could have just taken you away and then hired an army of lawyers to hold on to you."

Winnie got that stubborn look that I knew only too well. "I know, but I had to make sure he didn't find out the truth about Miss Drake."

"You took that risk because of me?" I asked.

"I had to keep you safe no matter what happened to me," she said.

A lump formed in my throat. "All the lawyers and thugs in New York couldn't keep me away from you."

Since Liza now knew where I lived, I asked her and Winnie to tea the next afternoon.

Liza immediately complimented my Bokhara. "What an exquisite carpet." She pointed to the splashes of paint. "And what an interesting design."

I glanced at Winnie and gave a harrumph. "There was an accident. I'm afraid I've been so busy that I haven't gotten around to having it cleaned yet."

As I started to serve the tea, Liza wondered, "What was Dad like as a boy?"

I set her cup and saucer down on the coffee table. "Your grandmother Mary spoiled him rotten, I'm afraid. He was her favorite."

Liza took the cup. "I would have thought Aunt Amelia would be the favorite. She was so sweet."

"Well, she was her father's favorite." I gave Winnie her tea. "But though Amelia was sweet, she knew her own mind." I like to think I had a paw in helping her become independent. "And your grandmother would've preferred a daughter who was a bit more moldable." Mary wanted a mindless little robot who always did what she was told to do.

When I set out the plate of Savoy cakes, Winnie cooed, "Ooh, ladyfingers."

I corrected her. "Technically, they're empress fingers. I received the recipe from Catherine the Great's pastry chef."

Winnie nibbled a cake. "Where was Cathy and what made her so great?"

Winnie didn't seem to be in awe of anyone or anything. "She ruled the Russian empire," I said, "and as for what made her great, ask Vasilisa."

Crumbs on her lips, Winnie whipped round to her mother. "What did I tell you, Mom? Miss Drake has been everywhere and done everything."

"You sound well traveled, too, Liza," I said, trying to change the subject.

Liza made a face exactly the way Winnie did. "Not by choice."

"We still had fun, though." Winnie began eating another cake.

After that, it was easy to keep Winnie and Liza talking about the happier moments from their adventures. Finally, we took the broken camera and flash drive into the kitchen, where I incinerated them in my kitchen sink.

During the crisis, Liza hadn't thought of buying Christmas presents, so she left now to begin shopping online, but Winnie stayed behind. I expected her to celebrate her triumph over her grandfather, but instead she seemed lost in thought.

I cleared my throat. "You're unusually quiet. Is something bothering you?"

"Granddad said I was ruthless—just like him," Winnie said. "But I don't want to be."

Even though she hadn't required me for her victory, Winnie still needed me! So I gave her a full dose of dragon comfort by wrapping a foreleg around her shoulders and coiling my tail around her waist and making her feel safe and secure.

"Every virtue has a flip side." I took care to pat her back with just the pad of my paw. "There's nothing wrong with being determined because you want to protect the ones you love. There is nothing right with being ruthless for selfish goals. So stop worrying. You're not like Jarvis. You're a 'plucky lass' just like Nessie."

Even though she squeezed me as hard as she could, I barely felt it through my armored skin. "I'll always watch over you, Miss Drake, even if it means I have to face a dozen granddads."

It was an odd moment for me, because I felt like we had traded places. In all my centuries of raising naturals, I had been the one to take care of my pets. Winnie was the first to protect me—as if I actually needed it.

Belatedly, I realized that a pet could be too clever for her own good, because she was smart enough to discover new ways of putting herself in danger. Still, she was also brave enough to face that danger, so I returned her embrace, using the lightest pressure. One must value courage, no matter how misguided.

CHAPTER SIXTEEN

*A wise dragon enjoys Christmas, when naturals
are at their least obnoxious.*

∾ Winnie ∾

December was like skating down the steepest part of Fillmore Hill. The days whizzed by, and all my tests, assignments, and school activities blurred together.

It was just as hard to keep track of all the holidays we were celebrating, like Hanukkah, Winter Solstice,

Christmas, and Kwanzaa. There were festivals I had never heard of, like Saskia's Chironia, which involved dancing something called the *gallopade*.

Life didn't slow down either when I got home. For several evenings in a row, Mom and I sat at the dining room table surrounded by boxes of sparkly holiday cards. Mom loved to add glitter to cards, so there was glitter on them, on the table, on the floor, and just about everywhere.

She was writing to all the friends we had made during our years avoiding my granddad's clutches.

I wanted to keep my promise to Granddad. I picked a card swimming in glitter and imagined him opening it with Magnus on his lap. Magnus would look very jolly covered with red and gold sparkles.

I wrote in my note that I had sold three of my playful otter drawings at the Spriggs holiday boutique. I told Granddad all the money we raised by selling handmade crafts and antiques was going to help sick children in Africa. That was something I was proud of, and too bad if he didn't approve of charity.

"I'm running out of things to say," I told Mom, and she shook her head sympathetically.

"Keep it short and sweet, then," she said. "Wish him health and good things in the New Year."

So I did . . . and I meant it, as long as he kept his distance. I sealed the envelope, stamped it, and I was done with card number one. Mom was already starting her fifth.

"Cookies, Madame? Little Madame?" said Vasilisa, bringing in a platter.

Just the thing to keep up our strength.

As soon as we had finished with the cards, it was time to put up the Christmas tree. It took Cullen and two of his helpers to get our Christmas tree into the house and set up in the parlor. It was a beautiful living tree and humongous—more than twice as tall as me. Mom and I would ask Cullen to plant it in a park after the holidays. It made sense to me. We would enjoy it now, and other families could enjoy it later.

Cullen planted his fists on his hips as he stared proudly up at the fir. "This is my biggest and finest tree. Only the best for my friend Miss Drake, the Grand Dame of the San Francisco Magicals." He scratched the back of his head. "Though I don't know what I'm going to tell those witches who wanted it for their Winter Solstice shindig."

"We don't want you changed into anything warty," Mom said in sudden alarm.

"Why not give them your second-best tree and

promise them some nice flowers for their midsummer party," Miss Drake suggested. "I'll pay for everything."

Cullen looked relieved. "That should make everything hunky-dory."

"Well, thank you, Cullen," said Mom politely. "It's an amazing tree."

But I saw her peek at our little old tree in its place on the massive fireplace mantel and smile. We couldn't help grinning whenever either of us looked at it. Dad had made it from salvaged branches, painted in bright greens and reds and gold. Then the three of us had cut animals from felt and made ornaments with pipe cleaners, walnut shells, and anything else our imaginations could transform. And as we laughed at each new creation, his laughter was loudest of all.

Dad's tree was art patchworked from simple things, much like our old life. But we had a new life now, with a new home of our own and new friends, and we needed a new tree to celebrate all that. So this year, we had two trees, to remember our past and celebrate the present.

After Cullen had left, we got to the fun of decorating. Vasilisa brought down several crates of ornaments from the attic. As we unwrapped and placed them carefully on the buffet, Miss Drake told us the story behind each one.

Some of them were crude angels made of twigs and

string but just as precious. Great-Grandfather Caleb and his parents had made them while they lived in a tent in a park after their home was destroyed in the Great Earthquake in 1906. Others were fragile painted balls as thin as bubbles and a glistening star covered in glass glitter, valuable antiques that Great-Great-Grandfather Sebastian had bought later in Bohemia.

When Vasilisa opened the box marked *lights,* I saw that Great-Aunt Amelia had a trillion wires and bulbs all jumbled together in the world's biggest knot.

Miss Drake cleared her throat. "Small Doll, if you please." By now, Mom knew about Small Doll too.

The next moment, the lights lay in neat coils.

Mom and I started forward, but Miss Drake told us, "This was always my job." And with a quick wave of her paws and a bell-like chant, the lines of bulbs rose upward like vines with colored berries. They danced in the air around the tree, snuggling evenly on the branches, wires hidden, the ends of each strand clicking neatly into the next.

Miss Drake dramatically took the last plug and fitted it into the socket. The tree glowed instantly with a rainbow of colors I had never seen before, changing into more amazing shades every moment and casting brilliant reflections across the ceiling.

Vasilisa clapped her hands together like she was five. "Lovely as always, Miss Drake," she said, and then looked eagerly at Mom. "Now you will decorate, Madame?"

I started to work on the lower half, and Mom and Miss Drake tackled the highest branches. But when it came to the crowning star, Miss Drake let me scramble up on her back. Then, with a gentle stroke of her wings, my dragon rose into the air. She hovered, her head brushing the ceiling, as I set the old sparkling star on the tippy-top.

Mom was right. It certainly was an amazing tree, and all around it was my ever so amazing family—Mom, Miss Drake, and our friends.

At that moment, I wished I had arms twenty feet long so I could hug them all at the same time.

Great-Aunt Amelia used to hold a holiday open house in December, though while she was ill, she hadn't been up to it. But Mom and I thought it was a lovely tradition, so we asked Miss Drake whom to invite and what to do.

Paradise took over decorating the outside. Pots of red and pink poinsettia and a herd of life-size grapevine deer greeted our guests. Many were neighbors I had seen and waved to on the way to school, and others were old friends of my great-aunt. Miss Drake, in her human form, wore a bright red sweater with white velvet trim and introduced everyone to Mom and me.

Mom had told me to invite my friends from school, and Mabli and Liri arrived together. Zaina's mother dropped her off, and Saskia jogged over the hills to be here.

"Just one more week of school, and we'll be on vacation. Then we won't see each other for two whole weeks," Liri said sentimentally. She was a softy.

It wouldn't be all hardship for her, though. Her family was going to Clear Lake up north.

"What're you doing during the holidays?" Mabli asked me.

"Oh, we haven't decided yet," I told her. All my friends had cool vacation plans, but none of them could compare to an adventure with Miss Drake, so I didn't want to rub it in.

"What's *she* doing here?" Saskia gasped.

In their matching lavender high-fashion outfits, elaborate hairdos and expensive makeup, Silana and Nanette looked as if they had just stepped out of a fancy department store window.

"I invited them," I said. After two weeks stuck with one another, I thought I should make the gesture to my frenemy. Mom hadn't been too sure about putting them on the guest list after Nanette had tried to make me disappear. I'd argued that if I could face Granddad in his hotel suite, we ought to be able to deal with Nanette in our own home. "But I never expected them to accept."

"Ms. Voisin, Nanette, how nice to see you," Mom called politely as she headed toward them.

I went over too. "Hey, you came."

"Not a bad tree," she said, jerking her head toward the live one. "But what's that funny-looking one?" She pointed at Dad's tree.

So much for the truce.

"We couldn't afford a real one for years, so my dad and I made it," I snapped.

But instead of making fun of me for being poor, Nanette said, "Oh, sorry." Then she gave a sad little laugh. "You know, I can't ever remember making anything with my dad."

"Well, he takes you on long trips." I added, "Sometimes."

Nanette raised an eyebrow. "If you're asking if I'm going to France after all, then the answer is yes. When I showed your invitation to Ms. Griffin, she told my father that we both seemed to be trying to get along. So he changed his mind about the trip."

"I'm glad it worked out," I said. "But let's not get stuck together again."

"Right back at you," Nanette agreed.

As the guests mingled in the parlor around the trees, Vasilisa and several of her cousins swept empty platters off the buffet and replenished them with new treats. Everyone ate and then ate some more, especially Cullen.

"How about some music now, Miss Drake?" Cullen called out. Earlier, he had lugged up stacks of music discs and her old Regina music box from the basement.

Miss Drake was kept busy changing discs to meet different requests. We all hummed or sang to the holiday songs and made space while Cullen danced to the jigs and hornpipes.

"This one's for the Spriggs girls," Miss Drake called, playing "Molly Malone."

We sang along, and then I raised my glass of sparkling cider. "To Nessie," I toasted.

And Mabli called out, "To Nessie and Spriggs."

I felt someone tap me on the shoulder. It was Nanette, who pointed to the window. "Look over there."

Beyond it, the bay glistened in the afternoon sun and on the glass itself I could see the reflections of my friends and me laughing and talking and having fun together. The only difference from the Magic Mirror scene was that Dad's tree and Nanette were here too. I guess I'd also changed that part of my future.

"I don't know what you did, but congrats," said Nanette. "You got the 'nice future' you wanted."

I grinned at my happy reflection and then at Nanette, and I knew she was right.

As the sun set, our guests began to leave, drifting down the driveway, past the deer, now bright with hundreds of white lights, to their homes.

"Well, Silana was on good behavior," said Miss Drake, sinking into the couch. "All the cookies disappeared, but none of the neighbors."

Mom settled next to Miss Drake and took her hand. "I felt like Aunt Amelia was here watching us."

"I wouldn't be surprised," said Miss Drake. "She never was one to miss a jolly time."

Dad had never been able to wait until Christmas Day to open his presents, so we'd always exchanged them on Christmas Eve. Mom and I unwrapped our presents in front of our old tree, sipping hot cocoa and toasting by the cozy flames in the fireplace. We set out a cup of cocoa and a bit of marshmallow for Small Doll, too, which disappeared in the wink of an eye.

Before Mom opened up my present, I told her to think of an angel. When she lifted out the silver egg in her palms, the ribbons of silver stars uncoiled and immediately transformed into a lovely creature with glorious wings.

"It's perfect for Dad's tree," she said, and then suddenly, since we both were thinking of him, the angel transformed into my dad's face. Mom gasped. I explained about Serpent Silver and how it had reflected our thoughts. She touched Dad's face and softly whispered, "He is always with me, Winnie." Then she looked at the tree, and the stars rearranged into an angel again. "Wherever did you get this?"

So I told her about the silkie fair.

"Miss Drake keeps telling me you're safe with her," said Mom. Though I could see a look of concern about my swimming deep under San Francisco Bay, she shook her head, grinned, and said, "And if you can't believe a grand dragon, then whom can you believe?"

Granddad had sent an enormous package to me, and I wondered if it was full of something sensible like a year's supply of socks. But when I opened it up, there were boxes and boxes of note cards . . . and a greeting from my grandfather.

Merry Christmas, Winifred, he had written by hand, a very shaky one. I could see the old man slowly forming each letter in his old-fashioned penmanship.

> *I thought you would like writing on these.*
> *I know I would like seeing these arrive in the mail.*
> *Best wishes,*
> *Grandfather Jarvis and M.*

To my delight, the cards had a raised golden image of the distinctive pennant on our house—three dragons rampant. My granddad had no idea how very fitting that was for me. I touched the very elegant letters of my name. My cards were just as pretty as Nanette's, and I thought even nicer.

"The notes are very elegant, and there must be hundreds of them." I could tell Mom was a bit unsure about the gift too. "I think you should take one box out and put the rest away. He can't expect you to write him that often."

I wasn't sure about that, but I liked her idea and I liked the cards too. And now I could write a proper thank-you to Miss Drake!

Under the tree, waiting to be given to Vasilisa and Paradise on Christmas Day, were packets of Liri's soothing bubble bath salts that I'd bought at the school's holiday boutique.

And in the trunk of Mom's car were five pounds of the highest-quality Belgian chocolate. Any chocolate candy inside the house was fair game for Small Doll—and at Halloween, Small Doll counted the front porch as part of the house, so she raided the trick-or-treaters' bags too. But Mom's car was off-limits.

Mom gave me a stack of gifts, some clothes, but mainly art supplies, nicer ones than I had ever had. Opening up the boxes of watercolors, pencils, and brushes, all new, untouched and clean, made my fingers tingle wanting to give them a try.

But first I wanted to give Miss Drake her present. "Mom, do you mind if I visit Miss Drake?"

"You should," Mom said. "And in the meantime, I'll take this moment to remember Dad." She touched the angel, and the silver pieces slid about until Dad's face was smiling again.

So I went up to my room and opened my closet. Inside was Miss Drake's present. It had been a job wrapping something that enormous in gold paper.

I'd been worrying what to get a dragon who can buy

anything with her pearls, but as soon as I saw it, I knew it was the perfect present for Miss Drake.

Back in the first week of December, Mabli and I had been storing donations for the white elephants' table at the Spriggs holiday boutique. She was putting a humorous plate of golfing warthogs on a shelf while I was adding a bag of yak-hair doilies to a plastic bin of linens, when I spotted the trunk next to me on the floor.

On the lid, someone had carved a map of the Seven Seas, while a mermaid swam on the front, and a slender octopus stretched her long curving arms around the back and one side. On the last side, the figure was worn away, but I could see that it was a dragon soaring above the waves. It was an amazing creature, just like someone I knew all too well.

Sir Isaac was pricing the items, and I called him over, in my nicest ready-to-bargain voice. "I'd like to buy this for a dear friend," I told him, pointing to the chest. "She's elderly, and I think it would please her. But it's not in very good shape."

He examined the chest inside and out. The tag had a question mark and a note reading *as is*.

"A sailor's sea chest," Sir Isaac called it. "And from its condition, I'd say it's traveled around the world once or twice, like your elderly friend. I'll concede that it's a bit scruffy, but mind you, every dent and chip was earned honorably during the owner's adventures. And whoever decorated it wielded chisel and hammer lovingly. So what will you offer for such a historical treasure, Burton?"

I knew that everything was going for a good cause, so I offered all the money I had. I was afraid it was worth a lot more.

"Since it's for your elderly friend," he said with a wink, "I'll exercise my judgment and call that a fair price." He even had a school gardener deliver it.

Later, in our garage, I cleaned and polished it with Vasilisa until our arms ached, but the wood was golden again and the brass fittings shined brightly.

"See, like new," Vasilisa said, smiling. "But it is a shame some of the carving was gone before you got it."

Yet even where it was worn-down, I could see what the wood-carver had planned, what he had imagined. So, with a touch of paint, of color and shadow, the octopus, mermaid, and dragon darted across the sides, full of life again.

It was a special box for a special dragon, and tugging it behind me now, I started for Miss Drake's.

Chapter Seventeen

A happy pet will make you feel five centuries younger.

⟶ MISS DRAKE ⟵

Thump, thump, thump.

When I heard the noise, I opened my apartment door. "If that's Santa's reindeer, you've taken a wrong turn. The roof is that way." I pointed at the ceiling of the basement.

"Nope, just one of his elves with a present for you." Winnie nodded to the large box wrapped in gold paper. "Ho, ho, ho!" she said in a deep voice. "Have you been a good little dragon this year?"

"I haven't heard anyone complain except for a certain urchin named Winnie." I stepped back. "But no one listens to her."

I'd decorated my home with holly and berries and branches of pine that scented the air as much as Winnie's live tree did. But Winnie ignored everything as she dragged the box onto the Bokhara. "Open it! Open it!"

"I can wait till tomorrow," I sniffed. "It's not Christmas yet."

She was fairly bouncing up and down with impatience. "So what? I can't wait to see your face when you unwrap it."

"But it's not proper. . . ." I held up my paws as she glared at me. "All right, all right, I was just joking." To tell the truth, I was dying of curiosity. The paper had torn slightly in several spots and what I saw intrigued me.

I was stunned after I ripped off the paper.

When I didn't say anything right away, Winnie grew worried. "Don't you like it? You said you were running out of room for tiaras in your old chest. Maybe you could start with the one you'll win at the Enchanters' Fair next year. . . ."

She stopped talking when I looked at her.

"You did this, Winnie?" I asked softly. "You painted the carvings for me?" When she nodded, I was still at a loss for words. "Well, I never . . . where did you find it?"

"At the holiday boutique," she answered. "Sir Isaac seemed to think I'd found a treasure." She watched me eagerly to see if I agreed.

Her face wreathed in a broad smile when I said, "You most definitely did."

I pointed to places on the map and told her of a battle with a giant octopus who had tried to drown me but ended up needing to regrow a few arms. And when I saw the sea-horse pendant that the mermaid wore, I was sure I knew her family.

"And I don't know how that sailor came to meet him," I said, "but that dragon is a definite likeness of my younger brother Alfie. Always a bit of a scamp, but my favorite nonetheless. His yarns must have inspired the sailor to carve these scenes."

Winnie relaxed then and plopped down into the armchair, relieved that her present was a success. "Will I ever meet your brother?"

I shrugged. "Who knows? As we dragons say, 'He goes wherever wind and tide take him.'"

I rose then and took the small seashell-shaped box

from the mantel. I hadn't expected Winnie to be worthy of this after just five months together, but then I had never expected her to face Jarvis alone—and I certainly never thought she could make him back down. But she had—and yet in such a way that they had become friends of a sort.

I'd asked Reynard's cockroaches about what had happened between Winnie and her grandfather, but they had been hiding because one of Jarvis's thugs had gone after them earlier with bug spray.

In the end, I'd had to trust my instincts. There might be smarter naturals and there might be happier naturals, but no natural had amazed me like Winnie. Of all my pets, I think she was going to be the most incredible— and the most challenging.

Turning, I held my present out to her on my paw. "My box is smaller than yours, but the treasure is inside."

"Ooh," she cooed in wonder when she lifted the lid. Taking out the gold ring, she held it between a thumb and finger as she studied the three thin round bands. Set in the center was a small purplish red stone surrounded by tiny balls of gold. It was very pretty, but far too large when she tried it on one of her fingers.

I took the ring back. "I need to be the one to do that

this first time." Then I intoned solemnly, "I who own this ring bequeath it to its new owner. May it protect her with all its power." Just as soon as I slipped it onto her middle finger, the gold bands shimmered and shrank slightly so that it was a snug fit.

"It's magic, isn't it?" Winnie asked excitedly.

I pointed at the gem. "Yes, it's a very special stone. Here under lamplight it's red, but when you wear it in daylight, it will change to a brilliant blue-green. But it's more than a pretty bauble. I've had this ring a very long time, and it's served me well. I gave it to your great-aunt, and she always wore it. But just before she died, she returned it to me. Now I want you to have it, and so would she."

"I've been wanting to do magic ever so long." Winnie extended her hand, studying the ring from different angles. "Will it let me fly? Will it turn me invisible? That would be so cool!"

"Not for me," I said firmly. "I don't want an imp like you sneaking up on me all the time and pulling my tail." I waved my paw. "When you're ready, I'll teach you how to use the ring." And before she could ask when that would be, I held up a paw. "But that will not be today. Nor tomorrow. Nor the day after that. It will be in the fullness of time."

Winnie hid her disappointment as she held the ring out at arm's length. "Well, in the meantime, I've got a real pretty ring."

She was taking things so well that I thought she deserved a second gift. So I unfolded my wings. "But if it's flying you want, there's nothing like a Christmas Eve flight."

Winnie leapt out of the chair. "Let's go!"

I called Liza to make sure it was all right. "Don't keep her out too late, Miss Drake" was her only condition.

By now, Winnie had bits of clothing and odds and ends squirreled around my apartment, so she was able to dress snug and warm during the flight.

Then, disguising myself as a human, we left through my tunnel, crossed from the park, and entered the hospital. The staff had decorated the lobby with tinsel garlands of green and red.

I gave a little cough. "Ahem. Since it's the season of sharing, I don't suppose you want to share the magic word with me?"

She started laughing. "Not a chance. I made a promise to keep it secret."

"Well," I asked, trying to sound as casual as I could, "I'll wager you didn't make a promise about Jarvis's box. What was inside?"

Winnie continued laughing. "Nope, that's part of the promise too. So you're not getting a peep out of me."

"I was afraid of that," I grumbled.

We rode the elevator to the roof then, where I changed myself back into a dragon.

The sky was clear, and I drank the cold air as if it were the elixir of youth. And when I exhaled, I felt all my worries drop from my shoulders along with the years.

The stars tugged at me with invisible strings just as they had when my family had taken me to the surface of the ocean to see the night sky for the first time. I'd only been a hatchling, but even then I'd yearned to soar up into it and beyond. So as soon as I felt Winnie clamber onto my back, I sprang from the rooftop.

Night flights are challenging over the sea or strange lands, but I've always loved flying over San Francisco after sunset. With their decorations and festive displays, the lighted streets seemed like jeweled ribbons wrapped around the biggest Christmas gift itself—the city. And I intended to unwrap it with Winnie.

So I soared out over the inky waters of the bay to the Bay Bridge, its outline dazzling in many thousands of white lights. I flew under the span, hearing the roar of traffic and the thump of wheels as they rolled from one section of the roadway to the next.

The tall clock tower of the Ferry Building greeted us, and the boxy high-rises near the Embarcadero were lit to look like enormous Christmas packages—a much cheerier view than their bland everyday one.

"There's Union Square!" shouted Winnie. "I can see the big tree." The fir looked as if it had been suspended in the middle of a pirouette, the lights on its sides like strings of fiery beads.

I soared higher and higher until the hills became small mounds and the cars crawled up their sides like bugs with glowing eyes. All of San Francisco's windows burned like fiery chips in some strange, lovely mosaic.

"It's like a fairyland," said Winnie, and I agreed. At night, San Francisco showed its magical self if you would look. So we enjoyed doing so, sweeping through the evening sky.

"I hope next year will be as much fun as this year," she said.

"Time will tell—whether we wish it or not," I told her.

That's something I've learned through the centuries. Things unfold and change in surprising ways. Last Christmas Eve I spent with Fluffy at home. I hadn't been looking forward to this year and saying good-bye to her. How could I have known that a new pet like Winnie would storm into my life and make things so interesting again?

Or how could she have known celebrating last Christmas on the run from her grandfather that this year she would have a home, a new school, new friends, and someone like me watching over her?

"Hold on," I said as I did a loop. The starry sky and the jewel-lit ground spun around and traded places for a moment.

"Yippppeeeee!" Winnie said. "Merry Christmas, Miss Drake."

"Merry Christmas, Winnie," I replied. "And many, many more to come."

As I turned slowly for home, I didn't need any magic mirror to see ahead to all the new adventures—and exasperating misadventures—that my all-too-clever pet would create for us. But as long as we could face them together, life would be as exciting as it would be delightful.

AFTERWORD

The Spriggs Academy is based very loosely on Joanne's and my educations. While none of our teachers flew or took us on field trips to meet Nessie, we did have teachers who could still tap-dance as they had once done on Broadway, and who in chemistry class would flash-freeze goldfish in liquid nitrogen and then revive them in water. Nor did they have a magic mirror, but they brought to life the great individuals from literature, mythology, history, and science. Ultimately, what they really taught us was to find delight in learning something new, and we've tried to have the Spriggs Academy faculty do the same for Winnie.

Sir Isaac Newton explored the world and all its physical phenomena with the same excitement with which Europeans investigated the new wonders of the American continents. He was as methodical in his attempts to find the philosopher's stone as in his attempts to understand the properties of gravity and light.

Nor was he alone in his search for the philosopher's stone. He corresponded with other great minds who were engaged in the same quest—people like Robert Boyle, who helped found modern chemistry, and John Locke, the influential philosopher. Sir Isaac pursued the philosopher's stone for twenty-five years, until he wrote in his notes that he had discovered "the stone of the ancients" and then quit his chemical studies.

We don't think he really found the stone, and there are other reasons he could have stopped his chemical experiments. But there are enough historical facts about the stone to spin them into fantasy.

If the philosopher's stone could have made Sir Isaac immortal, he would have handled the consequences with the same shrewd intelligence and systematic patience that he used in his scientific and mathematical inquiries, as well as his later successful pursuit of counterfeiters who were ruining the British economy. For his many achievements, he was knighted by Queen Anne.

For a description of Sir Isaac's search for the philosopher's stone, as well as his hunt for criminals, I would recommend Thomas Levenson's engaging book, *New-ton and the Counterfeiter.*

Both deep and long, Loch Ness contains more freshwater than any other lake in Great Britain . . . and some people believe a monster as well. They say the first re-corded sighting was in AD 565. Since then, the legends and stories about the creature whom fans have affection-ately named Nessie have grown. But despite numerous attempts, no one has been able to confirm Nessie's exis-tence scientifically.

Though Nessie's favorite tune, "Molly Malone," has be-come the unofficial anthem of Dublin in Ireland, it is gener-ally accepted that a Scot from Edinburgh, James Yorkston, wrote the song. It was first published in the 1880s.

As for the other historical references, Delphi was a sacred place in ancient Greece where games were held every four years, inspiring our modern Olympics. It was most famous, though, for the Oracle. But her prophecies were so ambiguous it was possible to misinterpret them. King Croesus of Lydia, in what is now Turkey, asked the Oracle if he should go to war with Persia. The Oracle re-sponded that if he attacked, a mighty empire would fall. King Croesus decided that meant he would be able to defeat the Persian Empire, but it was his own kingdom that was lost instead.

Catherine the Great ruled from 1762 to 1796. She had many great achievements and extended the borders of the Russian empire, including colonizing what became Alaska.

Kush was an ancient kingdom in what is now Sudan, but there is no colossus there nor wizard who created it.

The master of Laki is fictional, but there is a volcanic fissure in Iceland named Laki that erupted in 1783 and didn't stop until 1784.

As for the mythological figures, the most famous cyclops was Polyphemus, who trapped the Greek hero Odysseus and his crew so he could eat them. The Greek poet Homer described in *The Odyssey* how Odysseus escaped. Amphitrite's titles and powers vary, but she was a spirit of the sea who was married to Poseidon, the god of the sea. And Eurybia was a sea spirit with a flint heart.